Praise for

"The Door Within reminds us that there is much more to life than what we see before our eyes."

~Josh D. McDowell, Author of *More Than a Carpenter*

"Batson leads young readers to a fantasy realm where faith and sacrifice serve as essential tools in an epic battle between good and evil."

~*Publisher's Weekly*

"When I hand Batson books to my children, I know they will find high adventure, amazing courage, sacrificial love, and the ride of their lives."

~Bryan Davis, Author of *The Dragons in our Midst*

"Could the next Harry Potter be a devout Christian?"

~Jaqueline J. Salmon, *The Washington Post*

"There's a magical quality to Mr. Batson's writing, a reader can't resist turning the pages as he draws you in, weaving new worlds and imaginative characters into epic stories that are sure to captivate. His work is a definite staple in our family's library."

~Rachel Marks, Author of *Darkness Brutal* and *The Dark Cycle trilogy*

A CHRISTIAN'S CAROL

WAYNE THOMAS BATSON

This story is a retelling of the Public Domain work by Charles Dickens: *Dickens, Charles, 1812-1870. A Christmas Carol and Other Stories. New York :Modern Library, 1995. Print.*

All biblical references from: *New American Standard Bible.* La Habra, CA: Foundation Publications, for the Lockman Foundation, 1971. Print.

Quotation from Dr. Martin Luther King Jr.: King, Martin Luther, Jr. *Strength to Love.* [First edition]. Harper & Row, 1963. Print.

Editing by Laura G. Johnson of Red Pen Proofreading

Book Layout and Interior Design by Malachi Armas

Cover Main Artwork: Caleb Havertape Illustration

Cover Design and Layout: Wayne Thomas Batson

Wayne Thomas Batson
Writing Blog: www.enterthedoorwithin.blogspot.com
Contact for Author Events: batguy21784@yahoo.com
Twitter: @WayneBatson
Facebook: https://www.facebook.com/wayne.t.batson

DEDICATION

To the Friend of sinners whose love defeated death and fear,
this story is and always has been, Yours.

CONTENTS

PREFACE

I HAVE ENDEAVORED IN this Spirited little book, to pay homage to Dickens' classic tale while, at the same time, raising the specters of several more modern social issues that confront our society. In particular, this version attempts to explore how modern Christians often react in ways contrary to biblical teaching, especially towards our fellow man who lives a lifestyle outside our collective comfort zone.

A Christmas Carol has always been one of my favorite stories. No Christmas Eve passes in the Batson household without some version (if not several versions) of A Christmas Carol entertaining and encouraging us. I nearly always weep at the end because this story speaks a truth—His truth—that even a reprehensible villain like me might be rescued. For in this truth dwells The Hope of the Ages. In calling my version of the story "A Christian's Carol," I by no means wish to deter anyone from reading it. That said, there is (I hope) a reminder for the Faithful that will haunt our houses—and churches—pleasantly.

Your Friend and Servant,

W.T.B.

December, 2018

STAVE I

CHASTAIN'S GHOST

MARLEY CHASTAIN WAS DEAD to begin with. There can be no doubt whatever about that. No brain waves. No heartbeat. No reflexes. Clinically and categorically dead. Doctor Forbes Kennedy Greene, Chastain's family physician, put the time of death at 6:46 on the evening of December 24th, and made the dreaded phone call to Chastain's business partner, Ebenezer Krow. Of course, Krow, being a man of evidence and a legal mind insisted on confirming Chastain's demise.

Upon the stroke of midnight, Krow arrived at the Universal Medical Center of Manchester, New Hampshire. He found Chastain's body lying on a narrow bed in a tiny, severely sterile gray room on the sixth floor.

"He is dead, then," Krow said.

Dr. Greene, a harried man with a slightly hunched back and trembling hands, glanced over at the linen covered corpse as if to say, "Isn't it quite obvious? We doctors tend not to joke around about death."

But Krow would have none of it. He said, "Show me."

With a deepening scowl, the doctor went to the bedside and lifted the sheet, revealing Chastain's body from head to waist. "Mr. Chastain suffered a massive cascading shutdown of his vital organs. Brain, heart, lungs—all ceased to function. Since then, his body began to cool, what we call the death chill."

Krow tucked his cane under one arm and removed his black leather gloves. He took hold of Chastain's left hand. "Hmph, cold," Krow said, "like meat from the ice box."

"Without a beating heart," the doctor went on, "his no longer circulating blood followed the whims of gravity and has settled and pooled."

"He always had that sickly yellow skin," Krow observed. "But the blue and purple splotches are new." Krow was now working at Chastain's left hand with both of his own. Finally, he removed a silver pinkie ring with a blood red stone. It was the very ring Krow had given Chastain those many years ago at the founding of their lucrative partnership.

Krow gave a gravelly chuckle as he said, "Far too generous a gift, and he'll certainly have no use for it now." Krow swiftly slipped the ring onto his own finger and nodded for the physician to carry on.

"There's not much more to say, really. We knew it was going to be some day this week. There was nothing more we could do for him but numb the pain."

"Numb the pain," Krow muttered. "That was Marley Chastain's motto in life. There's no tavern in Manchester he hadn't haunted a dozen times. No bottle he'd not had as a guest in his always-stocked cabinet. No tobacco product, and, as you well know, no pain medications he'd not abused."

Doctor Greene nodded, swallowed, and then waited.

Krow said, "Every document must show his death as a result of natural causes, of course. The Chastain family will not have its name sullied by the excesses of this weak man."

Dr. Greene looked away and replied. "I will see to it."

"Good, good." Putting on his gloves once more, Krow asked, "Were there any last words?"

The physician blanched. "As you know, Mr. Chastain hasn't been conscious for a week, but...at the end, just as his breathing had become louder and more labored, Chastain cried out a scandalous curse which I would not repeat to you or anyone else, lest it scar my soul."

Krow winced. Chastain had always had a foul temper and mouth to match, but something about the report of his final moments bothered Krow exceedingly. He moved slowly to the head of the bed and stared at the face of his former partner. Chastain's mouth and jaw were contorted as if he'd been in agony at the end. *So much for numbing the pain,* Krow thought. Chastain's oft-broken nose was scaly and splotched. And, if it were possible, his huge eyes bulged larger beneath those heavy lids as if the orbs had swollen in death.

Krow blinked and took a watchful step back from the bed. "Did you see that?"

Dr. Greene squinted. "See what?"

"His lower lip," Krow said, his voice an octave higher than usual. "I...I thought I saw his lip move."

"I didn't see anything of the kind. Mr. Chastain is quite dead, I assure you."

But Krow was not to be assuaged. He stared at Chastain's bottom lip and waited. When nothing occurred, he lowered his ear to the dead man's mouth and waited again. There was no stir of air, no breath.

"There," Dr. Greene said, "you see? Nothing at all, but it is really quite common to be unnerved by—"

"Ebenezer."

The whisper sounded like a shout in Krow's ear. He jerked away. One of Chastain's eyelids rolled back like a window shade, and Krow was transfixed. The iris and black pupil of that bulbous eye were somewhat occluded by a milky-pale cataract, and the whites were full of streaks of blood-like red lightning.

Krow backed into a bank of medical instruments and

dropped his cane. He gasped, still staring at his partner's eye.

"Relax, Mr. Krow," Dr. Greene said. "That's perfectly normal. It's the size of his oculus, his...his eyeball—the lids have popped open like that at least six times tonight. Look here." He flipped the power switches of two machines.

Krow picked up his cane and backed toward the door. Greene reached out to steady the man, but Krow recoiled and kept a careful distance between them.

Dr. Greene shrugged and went on to explain, "This is the heart rate monitor. You see? Flatlined. And this, this is the EEG. Zero brain activity. Marley Chastain is dead, has been dead for nearly six hours now."

"Natural causes," Krow growled. He lunged forward and held his walking cane dangerously close to the doctor's chin. The sharp beak of the cane's nickel-plated crow's head was a scant few inches from the doctor's jugular. "I won't take your word for it, Dr. Greene. My partner's reputation must be completely protected. Natural causes—I want copies of every document delivered to my office by noon tomorrow."

"Tomorrow?" Dr. Greene balked. "But tomorrow is Chris—"

"Tomorrow, by noon," Krow said, backing away but still pointing his cane menacingly. "You know I have friends above you—far above you. If you wish to continue practicing in this hospital, you'll do as I bid."

Dr. Greene's hunch deepened. "I will see to it," he said.

With a swish of his great coat, Ebenezer Krow turned to leave. The cadence of his boots and cane increased rapidly. *Thump-click, thump-click, thump-click.* Never once did Krow look back. He'd seen enough of Chastain and that grotesque eye.

"Hogwash," Krow muttered aboard the elevator. After decades of thumbing his crooked nose at excess and time, Marley Chastain, the renowned man of business had most assuredly been murdered by them both.

So at last, at the ripe—and I do mean, very ripe—old age of 88, Marley Chastain was dead. Dead as a cemetery stone.

The mention of a cemetery stone brings me back to emphasize the original point of salience: there was no doubt that Marley Chastain was dead. And this must be wholly understood or little grace will come from the harrowing tale I am about to unfold.

*   *   *

Krow never ordered a new sign for his firm, nor did he change a word on their websites, apps, stationery, or business cards. The firm was ever known as Krow and Chastain, and so it remained for these seven years after the death of Krow's partner.

Krow knew the value of a brand just as he knew the value of hard work; his hallmark virtue if the extent to which he took it could still be loosely connected to anything morally upright. Oh! But he was a violent crack of the whip, Krow! A pushing, prodding, scolding, chiding, judging, demanding, old legalist. Rigid and scraping as a chisel, from which no gladsome craft of wood would ever delight from its making; suspicious, and self-absorbed, and as watchful as a vulture. The bile within him bit at his old features, chafed his pointed nose, shredded his sunken cheeks, crippled his gait; made his wrinkle-nested eyes narrow, his tiny mouth thin, and spoke out caustically in his acidic voice.

Lauded as a holy terror in court, Krow spent his days—and nights—with his eyes glued to one of his many monitors or prowling through hefty law books. He carried the same reputation in church, especially to any of the more liberal congregants. Within the hallowed halls of St. Nicodemus Church of the Holy Ghost, Krow had ascended to the rank of Elder and earned the reputation as an authority in Old Testament Law. There, as in the courtroom, Krow raked great pleasure from wrecking the so-called logic of any who dared to debate him. He loved the robes and accoutrements of his office, as well as the grudging respect of his fellow elders. But more than all of that, Krow coveted the trepidation his very presence induced in most parishioners. After each service it was not uncommon for the Elders to disperse into the congregation to shake hands and offer pleasantries to the faithful. Krow need not worry about shaking hands, for the fearful flock—especially the children—gave him a wide berth all the way to the church doors. And usually, the effect continued out in the teeming masses of Manchester.

But what did Krow care? It was the very thing he liked. Bulling his will and his way to control every aspect of his life and that of others while, at the same time, warning the world to keep its hands off and warm embraces far from Ebenezer Krow.

Once upon a time—of all the splendid days of the year, on Christmas Eve—old Krow sat in his expansive office on the first floor of what was formerly the Ash Street School and put the finishing touches on an email about billable hours that was sure to disturb his new clients. But Krow wasn't so busy as to neglect keeping an eye on one of his legal clerks, Robert Craggett who had the galling habit of stealthily raising the thermostat a degree or two.

"Mr. Craggett!" Krow rasped, freezing Craggett in the very act.

"I'm sorry, sir," Craggett replied, easing back into his chair at his desk and positioning himself such that his computer's monitor hid his face from his employer.

"Come here, Mr. Craggett!"

The clerk obeyed and placed himself a few paces back from Krow's massive black walnut desk. Krow stood and reached for his cane, but it had fallen just out of range, so he pointed a long finger over his desk.

"Mr. Craggett," Krow said, "who pays the bill for heating this old building?"

"You do, sir."

"And who controls the temperature at all times?"

Craggett swallowed, and his very large Adam's apple bobbed. "You do, Mr. Krow."

"Lastly but most importantly, who maintains your contract and pays your salary?"

"You again, sir."

Krow crossed his arms. "Then, tell me, Mr. Craggett, why do you persist in this costly game?"

"Well, sir, like you said, sir: the building is very old. It's drafty. And on a raw, sleeting day like today, the cold seeps through the walls."

"Just as the heat seeps through the walls to the outside," Krow remarked. "From here on, Mr. Craggett, I have the perfect solution. For every time you raise the thermostat, I will deduct ten percent from your billable hours."

"Ten percent," Craggett replied, his voice failing. "But that would put me—"

"Ten percent per degree," Krow cut in. "More than reasonable to offset the rise in heating costs you cause. But, this need not happen, Mr. Craggett, if you'd simply do as the rest of this firm's employees do: dress for the temperature!"

"Yes, sir."

"Now, back to your duties, unless you'd prefer to work late this evening."

"No, sir," Craggett mumbled as he retreated. "Er...I mean yes, sir, I'll get back to my duties."

"See that you do."

Craggett was no sooner back at his desk when the office door opened with a swirl of sleet and snowflakes, and a ruddy-faced man with a mop of curly red hair entered.

"Merry Christmas, Uncle! God bless you!" he cried in a cheery voice. It was Krow's nephew, Fred Bithywell, and the way he flew into the office—almost on the wings of winter wind—gave Krow quite a start.

Krow regained his composure, glanced up from his monitor with one eye, and grunted, "Bah! Hogwash!"

Fred grinned, patted Craggett on the shoulder, and launched himself toward Krow's desk. "Christmas, hogwash, Uncle? I'm sure you don't mean that."

"I do," said Krow. "The way so many celebrate Christmas—you among the rest—no longer bears any resemblance to the austere event that it was. Santa Claus, trees, presents, gluttony—it's all hogwash. Merry Christmas! Commercial, wasteful Christmas is more like it."

"Ah, Uncle," the nephew returned jovially, "expecting coal in your stocking again this year, are you?"

"If only something so useful," Krow replied.

"Really, Uncle? So cynical."

"What else can I be?" Krow asked, slamming shut a book of law. "We live in a world of debauchery, and Christmas has become the chief festival of excess. The stores start flaunting their Christmas decorations and gift ideas in October! Why? Because gullible idiots gobble it all up. What is Christmas time but a time for spending money you don't have for things you don't need; a time for sloth, drunkenness, and every other deadly sin—all neatly tied up with green and red bows? If I could work my will, every fool who falls for a worldly Christmas should be strangled with his own strands of colored lights and then roasted slowly over a bonfire of wrapping paper, plastic Santas, and felt stockings. I'm quite serious."

Fred blinked. "I do believe that is the most disturbing notion I've ever heard. Uncle!"

"Nephew!" Krow thundered. "You keep Christmas in whatever way seems good to you. Let me keep Christmas as it should be kept."

"But you don't keep Christmas," the nephew replied. "You give it away."

"It seems to me that you gave Christmas away many years ago, along with any semblance of morality."

Fred's ruddy cheeks reddened with anger and he started to cross his arms. But at the last moment, he let out a deep breath, dropped his arms, and relaxed his posture. "I'll excuse your ill words, Uncle," he said, "and keep my good humor. Perhaps you're right. I no longer attend your church, nor do I adhere to your church's dreary outdated concepts. But I have found that Christmas time—even in the midst of the most gaudy decorations and silly customs—is noble time, a time when all of the world wishes good cheer upon one another; a time when petty judgments and conflicts are put aside in exchange for charitable peace. Say what you wish about Christmas; but I say, God bless it."

From behind the monitor across the room came the sound of loud applause, a raucous whistle, and a hearty "Hear, hear!"

"Let me *hear* any more from you, clerk," Krow warned, "and you'll keep your Christmas here in the office!" He turned back to his nephew. "That is the second time you've mentioned God's blessing. It's a wonder you're not preaching in one of those liberal churches downtown."

"Uncle Ebenezer," pled the nephew, "cannot we at least reconcile for a Christmas meal? Come tomorrow and dine with us."

Krow stiffened. He made fists of his hands, and his knuckles cracked. "Dine...with you? I'd sooner dine in hell first."

"But why?" Fred cried out. "Why?"

"Why did you get married?" Krow demanded.

"Because I fell in love."

"Because you fell in love," Krow mocked. "With a man? Don't you know how hideous that is in the sight of the Almighty?"

"Are you certain you don't mean in your sight, Uncle? There may actually be a difference. Come now, I'm not asking you to approve of my relationship with Kevin. I'm simply asking you to remember we are family. My mother, God rest her saintly soul, would want us to share Christmas together."

"Good afternoon," Krow said.

"I am sorry to find you in such a state on Christmas Eve. But, for another year, I've made this attempt at familial companionship, and I'll keep my Christmas spirit to the last. So, Merry Christmas, Uncle!"

"Good afternoon," Krow growled.

"And a happy New Year!"

"Good afternoon!" Krow practically yelled, but his voice was strained and hoarse.

Fred spun on his heel and, before he left the office, he stopped to wish season's greetings to Craggett who returned them warmly.

"There's another fool," Krow muttered, "my clerk on his salary and a wife and family inundated with medical bills, talking about a *Merry Christmas.* I'll be locked in a padded cell!"

The fool walked Krow's nephew to the door and, in the process of letting him out, let two other people in: a man and a woman, portly but dressed well in both form and purpose for the icy weather outside. They wore broad smiles and carried leather-bound tablet computers. As he stepped a little farther into Krow's office, the man removed his hat. Both visitors bowed politely toward Craggett who, feeling quite undeserving of such reverence, smiled nervously and nodded back.

The woman opened her tablet, and the light from its screen lit up a face already alight with mercy and passion. Her eyes were aglow with kindness and wit, and she said, "Krow and Chastain, I believe, Criminal Defense and Personal Injury Law."

The two visitors bowed again at Krow's approach, but Krow did not return with any gesture whatsoever, save steadily narrowing eyes.

The dark-skinned man with his hat in hand had a pleasantly booming voice when he asked, "Have I the pleasure of meeting Mr. Krow or Mr. Chastain?"

"Mr. Chastain has been dead seven years," Krow replied. He blinked reflectively. "He died seven years ago on this very night."

"My condolences on what must be a somber anniversary," said the man. "We have no doubt that Mr. Chastain's generosity is shared all the more by his surviving partner."

It certainly was, for Chastain and Krow had both been cut from the same scratchy woolen cloth. At the word "generosity," Krow actually recoiled as if ducking a blow.

"At this charitable, giving time of year," said the African-American woman, sliding her fingers across her tablet screen, "those of us with means find our hearts more open to the poor and needy."

The man put his hat under his arm and said, "We represent two charities: The New Hampshire Food Bank and Good Shepherd Inner City Provisions."

"Being a man who has suffered loss at this time of year," the woman said, "you understand that the poor and hungry who suffer every single day, suffer more around the holidays, especially on Christmas."

The man began again, "Many thousands try to weather the cold in makeshift cities made of tents and cardboard boxes and are in sore need of clothing, blankets, and food—for survival. Hundreds of thousands lack any of the comforts that we often take for granted, sir."

"Are there no shelters?" Krow asked.

"Many shelters," the man replied, "filled to bursting."

"And the group homes?" Krow pressed. "Are they still available at need?"

"They are," returned the man, "understaffed and terribly underfunded."

"The church soup kitchens and post-prison educational programs are operating as intended?" Krow inquired.

"Both very busy, sir," the man replied, closing the leather cover of his tablet.

"Oh, I was afraid from your pitiful descriptions that something had happened, stopping them all from fulfilling their duties," said Krow. "I'm relieved to hear your confirmation."

"You understand," said the woman, "the need is far greater than these establishments can provide. It is Christian cheer and provision for both mind and body that is in short supply. A few organizations like our own are working hard to raise a fund to provide the poor and destitute with food, drink, warmth, and counseling. We choose this time because loss and want, despair and shame are more keenly felt while, in the private sector, there is even greater abundance. What amount can we put you down for?"

"Do not put me down for anything," Krow replied.

"Ah, a true Christian giver," she said. "You wish to give anonymously."

"I wish to be left to my own devices," said Krow. "Since you ask for my wish, that is it. I do not make myself any merrier at Christmas than I do throughout the live-long year. I cannot afford to make idle people, most of them ex-prisoners and drug addicts, merry. Through my faithful tithing at St. Nicodemus for thirty years and my paying of more and more exorbitant taxes each year, I support all of the establishments I spoke of a moment ago. Those who are so needy must seek out such places."

The woman tilted her head sideways, and her mouth dropped open, but she found no words to say.

"These are not all ex-prisoners or drug addicts," the man said. "We're talking about the sick, elderly, and mentally broken—many can't go where you would have them. We're talking about good men and women who can't find work. We're talking about unwed mothers and abandoned youths. Many would rather die than be lost in the system."

"Well, if they would rather die," said Krow, "perhaps, they should then, and remove the excessive drain on civil society once and for all."

"Excessive drain on—!" the woman blurted. "I don't know who you think you are, mister, but—"

"Easy, Lucille," the man said, putting out an arm of gentle restraint.

But Lucille strode up to Krow, nearly bumping him. "You don't want to give? That's fine. But we're talking about human beings here!"

"Good afternoon," Krow said, turning his back to her and retreating to his desk.

"I ought to slap some sense into that man, Clinton," Lucille said, breathing heavily.

Clinton put his arm around Lucille and escorted her toward the office door. "Can't expect him to know anything about human beings," he said in a low but resonant voice, "'cause obviously he isn't one."

Krow watched them leave and then found Craggett watching him. "Back to work, Craggett!" Krow fumed, and he too returned to his work.

The old bell tower of Saint Marie Church on the west side of Manchester became enveloped in dreary mists and sheets of sleet but, as hours passed, the bell tolled on as resonant as ever.

At last, the time came for shutting down the office. Krow reluctantly powered down his computer and bank of monitors.

When he looked up, he saw that Craggett had already closed down his desk and put on his overcoat.

"Anxious to leave, are you?" Krow inquired pointedly.

Craggett threw a scarf around his neck and froze. "Well, sir, it is Christmas Eve," he said, "and my family is waiting."

Krow hastened to his clerk's desk, boot and cane *thump-clicking* all the way. "I suppose you'll want all day tomorrow, then?"

"Yes, sir," Craggett replied. "I put in for leave three months ago."

"How convenient," Krow sneered. "What if I told you that Anderson and Berkhart are both working tomorrow, trying to get ahead on the Donovan malpractice suit? Holiday pay is double time, you know."

"Yes, sir, and thank you for the opportunity, sir, but it's Christmas. Only once a year."

"A poor excuse for abandoning one's post," Krow observed. "Especially in such a vital time as this, but...I suppose your priorities aren't that of a true man of business."

"But, Mr. Krow," Craggett said, "you're a Christian man. Christmas is a high holiday. Won't you be celebrating tomorrow as well?"

Krow cleared his throat and buttoned his coat up to his neck. "I believe you heard the conversation I had with my sentimental nephew."

"Yes, sir."

"Then, you understand that Christmas is no excuse to avoid work. I will be here with the morning light, with Anderson and Berkhart, upholding the name of our fine firm. I'll expect you all the earlier the next morning."

The clerk agreed that he would; and Krow walked out into the fog with a guttural "Bah!" The mist was so thick and the night so dismal that Krow nearly walked over a little boy.

"Whoa, now!" Krow exclaimed, dancing awkwardly to avoid knocking into the child.

The boy's eyes were wide and bright, amber-brown even in the murk. He had absurdly curly brown hair, flecked with sleet and wore a smile so broad that it stretched his bluish lips thin. Krow noted that the boy was pale and gaunt, bore a crutch under each arm, and wore some kind of metal harness around his legs. The boy inquired, "You're Mr. Krow, aren't you?"

"Yes, yes, I am," he replied. "What's a boy doing out so late at night?"

"Little Bear!" Craggett sang out, gliding on the icy walk to scoop up the boy.

"Merry Christmas Eve, Big Bear!" the boy cried out, crushing Craggett's neck with his arms.

"Merry Christmas Eve, indeed!" Craggett replied. "But what are you doing out here? It's late and cold."

"I haven't been waiting long," the boy replied. "Mom let me take the bus to surprise you!"

"Well," said Craggett, "this day just keeps getting better. And, Tom, hear this: I have the whole day off tomorrow! And do you know who we have to thank?" Holding Tom lightly in the crook of one arm, Craggett turned and said, "Mr. Krow here. He's the one we have to thank."

"Hurrah for Mr. Krow!" Tom said. "Thank you, sir!"

"Pray, don't mention it," Krow spluttered out. "This your youngest, then, Bob?"

"That's right," the clerk replied. "Tom Craggett and six years old. Seven in January."

Krow's jaw worked busily. "Well, I'm sure you'll both be wanting to get along home. Lock up, then."

"Yes, sir," Craggett replied. Still holding Tom in his arm, he let the last of the employees file out and then activated the building's comprehensive alarm system: motion detectors, cameras with night vision, and endless digital recording that could be monitored in real time from anywhere in the world.

Krow watched over his clerk's shoulder, muttered something incoherent, and then disappeared into the icy night.

Craggett slipped and slid the entire journey to the bus stop with Tom whooping and cheering all the way. Once inside, out of the cold, they watched the sleet fall through the bus window. "Forecasters say it might turn to snow," Bob said. "Wouldn't that be marvelous?"

Tom's eyes glimmered when he replied, "It would be a Christmas miracle."

* * *

Krow walked a block to The Bleak House (his favorite tavern), and ordered his usual meal, "a boiled dinner," as it was called. The steaming pot arrived in no time, and Krow set to it. The corned beef brisket swam in an ocean of root vegetables, flanked by a few slices of limp cabbage. It was hearty and hot, if not tasty, and Krow liked it because the whole lot turned to a kind of salty mush that was easy on his teeth.

While slurping a rather brave spoonful, Krow became distracted by a cascade of raucous cheers from the bar. So loud were they that Krow spilled half the spoonful down his chin. Angrily patting up the moisture with a cloth napkin, Krow glowered at the inconsiderate gathering.

It was as an eclectic a group as Krow had ever seen: mostly young men and women but some in business attire, others in casual jeans and sweats, while still others looked as if they'd just drifted in from a local punk rock club. Nose rings, outlandish haircuts and colors, studded black leather jackets strewn with studded black leather belts—and makeup! Krow found himself studying a person with thick black eyeliner, bruise-colored eye shadow and blush, and rather vivid red and green lipstick. Top lip, green. For all the world, Krow could not decide whether he was looking at a man or a woman. Either way, Krow decided the being was most unpleasant to behold.

And the way the whole group was carrying on: slapping each other on the back, embracing, kissing, laughing, singing, and drinking—Krow couldn't understand why the tavern's manager hadn't already put a stop to it.

This is a public establishment, thought Krow. *People should be more considerate.* The man muttered another, "Bah!" and went back to his boiled dinner.

Now, it was a fact that The Bleak House was a very old tavern, but there was nothing particularly strange or eerie about it. It is also a fact that Krow's boiled dinner, while briny and somewhat bland, was still steaming hot. Let any man explain then, if he can, how such a settling of cold came over old Krow at that table in that tavern.

It began upon his left side as if someone had held open the tavern door a bit too long, letting in the seeking, searching, scratching wind. And yet the entrance to the pub was on Krow's right, and a great crackling blaze burned merrily in the fireplace not twenty feet to Krow's left.

Invisible tendrils of ice nipped Krow's arm, then his shoulder, and the man shrugged and rubbed to attain some warmth... in which course, he failed.

Krow looked about the room, peering through the vapors of his meal. No one else seemed to notice anything out of the ordinary. In fact, the group at the bar had just begun a spirited rendition of "The Twelve Days of Christmas," each person taking on a part and then all howling out the chorus.

The cold on that side intensified and, trembling mightily, Krow tried scooting across the bench seat as far as he might without losing the ability to tend to his dinner. But it was no good. The creeping chill followed.

Three things happened all at once: the rowdy group at the bar reached "Six Geese a' laying," the fumes over Krow's boiled dinner coalesced into a hideous, scowling face, and an absolutely chilling breath of air assaulted Krow's neck.

The man stood up abruptly, rattling his meal, and fled to the bar. "Chastain," he muttered, for though the vaporous face had been in a sickly state of decay, it could be none other than Marley Chastain.

Krow cast about the bar, looking for the keeper but saw that he had left his post to attend to a table on the other side of the room. Krow thought about rushing to the man, but somehow, sitting at the bar had removed the pervasive chill. And yet, still he trembled.

"Hey, there, you okay?"

At the voice, Krow jumped up. He turned to find one of the rowdy group, a woman with hair so dark a red as to be a kind of crimson-purple, staring at him with concern written all over her green eyes and darkling expression. In fact, the entire group seemed intent on Krow at the moment. He hadn't even heard them end their song prematurely.

"I...I'm fine," Krow muttered, glancing back at his table and the still steaming pot. "A chill, that's all."

"Are you sure?" the woman asked. "I saw you jump up over there, and you're shaking."

"Fine, I said," Krow grumbled. "Just need to pay for my meal and get home."

The gender-unclear being with all the makeup, leather, and spikes leaned toward the woman and whispered something in her ear. The woman nodded and said to Krow, "Hey, why don't you join us for a little while? This isn't a night to be alone on, Christmas Eve and all."

Krow turned and really took them all in. Eclectic really wasn't the word. Motley or disparate, perhaps. How such a group had ever come together as friends, Krow couldn't fathom. Why, some of them looked as if they might be a good fit for Krow's firm. And yet others looked disheveled or even indecent. One of the women at the corner of the bar wore a V-neck sweater that was far too tight and far too revealing. Krow averted his eyes.

"No," Krow said bluntly. "I was just leaving, and I have a full day tomorrow."

"Ah, don't we all?" the woman said. "Christmas parties, meals, travel—it's lovely, but it's a load."

Krow felt a trickle of sweat descend down the back of his neck, under his collar, and between his shoulder blades. "Not what I meant," he said. "I have a full day of work."

"Work?" echoed one of the group, a dark-skinned man in a

handsome suit. "What sort of bum would make a man work on Christmas Day?" This elicited a laugh from the whole group.

Krow sneered. "The sort of *bum* who believes undue celebration is sloth! I am my own boss, and I won't have it."

"Oh, dear," the woman said, sitting down beside him. "You really are wound quite tight. Here, why don't you hang with us a bit? We'll help you unwind. First pint is on me. What do you say?"

Krow felt warmer still. Uncomfortably warm. His neck began to itch. "I said 'No' and I mean no. Besides, I don't drink beer or any alcohol except for medicinal purposes."

"We all drink for medicinal purposes," said the man in the suit, causing a fresh peal of laughter.

"Look at you all!" Krow stammered. "What business do you believe you have with one another?"

The group went silent and, for a moment, the fire crackling was the only sound. But Krow wasn't finished. "You," he said, pointing in turn to those of the group in business attire. "Think you'll end up lifelong friends with them?" He pointed to the punk rockers and the underdressed woman. "You're all young but foolish, but soon enough, you find the lines are hard. And these ne'er-do-wells will be a drain on the lot of you."

"Did he honestly just say, 'ne'er-do-wells?'" asked the male or female being in a voice that confounded Krow's definitive efforts all the more.

The woman stood up and tossed half a pint of beer on Krow. "Here we are putting out a hand in kindness," she said, "and you judge us? You intolerant pig!"

Rapidly taking up napkins from the bar and wiping his face and clothes, Krow was far from daunted. "Yes, yes, I do judge you," he growled. "I've lived a long life and I've seen this world rotting more and more. Now, you live by the religion of 'if it feels good, do it!'" Krow saw tears in one woman's eyes and realized she was gripping the hand of another woman. "Disgusting. Men with men; women with women—some of you are so poisoned you can't tell what you are anymore."

Amid profanity-laced shouts and threatening gestures, a hand on Krow's left shoulder shut him up, and the bartender stood before him at last. "I think you need to leave," he said, his voice menacing.

"The very thing I want to do," Krow said, slapping a twenty onto the bar and marching toward the door. "Sick, I tell you," he said, "you're all sick."

Without a single look back, he lunged out into the pelting sleet and made his way west on Pearl Street. The winds stiffened, wailing and howling and fighting Krow for every step toward his home. Snow began to mix with the sleet, but the blend played the devil with Krow's vision. He could scarcely see the Binge-water Insurance storefront across the street, much less Walnut Street, yet a few blocks away. The usual *thump-click* of Krow's gait became more of a *splat-click*, for slush lay in viscous pools on both sidewalk and street.

Past the corner of Pearl and Beech, there was a side street Krow knew that would bring him behind his home. It wasn't really a shortcut, but it provided more immediate relief from the storm's teeth. Krow took it and, gratified by his wise decision, began to walk more quickly. Buildings with blank windows lined both sides of this unnamed alley, and its perennial darkness was broken only by three old street lamps on Krow's side of the street.

Snow and sleet came down handsomely in the light of those lamps, but as Krow passed by the first, there came a distinct buzzing followed by a sound like snapping sticks. The light went out. Krow stopped and stood there blinking, the darkness deeper with the light's sudden extinguishing. Krow gave the lamppost a few smart whacks with his cane, but the light remained out.

His heart beating a little faster, Krow ambled on toward the next street lamp. Upon his first step into its cone of illumination, the lamp abruptly went dark. Startling Krow even more, the light behind him came back on. This development played the very deuce with Krow, and he looked about, scanning the black windows for some sort of answer. Then, the gears and wheels of evidentiary jurisprudence began to move in Krow's mind. "It's those hooligans from my tavern," he muttered, glaring at the second story windows, one after the other. He saw no sign of movement, no sign that he himself was being observed. And yet, prank it must be, Krow thought.

"So be it," Krow said aloud, "have your fun. You'll not alter my path!" He said this with growing confidence, for his turn was only one street lamp away. But, Krow did not speed his steps. Slowly, with watchful deliberation, he advanced. And so it was that when he glanced through the snow, sleet, and shadow, across the alley, he caught his own reflection in the hardware store's window.

It was not a becoming image, for it was distorted by the ice and snow and seemed to show him much more bent and hobbled than he actually was. Krow continued on, but kept his eyes on those windows. And in just a few strides, the image changed. In his reflection, Krow seemed to be carrying something...and dragging something at the same time. Krow could not tell what it was, but tried to blink it away, to no avail.

And then, just behind him in the reflection, a mist of white sprang up. Krow quickened his pace then. Another burst of white bloomed, followed by a mysterious flickering shape.

"Daah!" Krow cried out, turning to look behind himself. There was nothing there but shadows and glistening pavement. The next street lamp was just ahead and, in spite of his recent experiences, Krow made for its light. But though he fought it, he could not resist looking at the reflection. There he saw himself once more, carrying something and dragging something, but the pale mists that had kindled were changing, taking on recognizable forms: limbs, torsos, heads, and faces—all enveloped in vapors.

Krow let out another cry, for the faces were grim and scowling and staring straight back at him. The flickering blotch vanished from the back of the train and reappeared directly behind Krow. Its glare was the most frightening, for its eyes were red. But its position was contested as one of the other forms replaced it in a blink, sending the former to the middle. They shuffled, blinking in and out and changing position until the last window.

Krow panted gusts of breath as he settled himself beneath the street lamp, which remained illuminated. *Get a hold of yourself*, Ebenezer, he thought urgently. *You need sleep. That's all.*

With a splitting crack, the light went out. Krow fled west in the dark, fearing that he was no longer the victim of a prank, but of a very great and imminent threat. Every sense told him he was being followed, chased even. He raced ahead, stumbling and tripping, his cane glancing off of uneven cobbled stone until, at long last, he reached the tall black wrought-iron gate that surrounded his home. His gloved hand flew to his coat pocket and withdrew a hefty key ring.

He rattled through the ring, found the right key, and slammed it into the lock. He was through with the gate locked behind him in an instant. From the perceived safety of that wrought iron, Krow stared out into the alley, expecting to see the trio of reflected phantasms career around the corner after him. No such thing occurred, and the street lamp was aglow as usual without so much as a blink.

Krow brushed a rime of snow and sweat off his brow, adjusted his coat, and made his way to the front of the house. Krow had picked up the mortgage of the recently renovated old Victorian from Chastain's family, for the man lived there for a great many years, and Krow had envied him for being so close to the firm.

It was a tall and boxy, turreted thing, originally built in 1843 as an orphanage. As such, it had a great many rooms— great rooms and sub rooms—parlors, living rooms, offices, and one very large, very dank basement. Krow did not want his old partner's room but instead chose a suite on the third floor overlooking Walnut Street.

After his most recent experience, Krow couldn't get to that room and its massive four-poster bed fast enough. Careful on the icy steps, Krow made his way to the front door, a vast and heavy thing made from imported leadwood. *No one would break that door down, not without a wrecking ball,* Krow had always thought. And he had augmented the entryway and the entire structure with state-of-the-art security systems.

Twin spotlights shone down upon Krow and two flanking cameras recorded his every move. He opened a narrow panel box on the right, and leaned forward so that the retinal scanner could confirm that he was indeed Ebenezer Krow. The high definition display blinked on, showing Krow a mirror image of his own eye with rotating ring graphics moving around his iris and pupil, both clockwise and counterclockwise.

"What's taking so long?" Krow muttered. He blinked and then stared. Something about the display image of his eye was changing. A pale cataract grew, millimeter by millimeter, occluding his eye like a swiftly forming polar ice cap. Vivid red capillaries shot through every bit of the whites. This was not Krow's eye.

"Chastain!" Krow exclaimed, staggering back from the device. The floodlights turned off, and there, hovering over the control panel like a ghostly three-dimensional portrait, was the face of his seven-year's dead partner, Marley Chastain. He wore a blank expression, and his eyes were fixed. The considerable wrinkles on his forehead were deeper than Krow remembered, now shadowy crevasses on that bold forehead. And the horn-rimmed glasses that he always wore were turned up upon the top of his head. His stringy hair moved about on its own like sea grasses in a relentless tide. All of this, every detail of Chastain's head and face, glowed pallid green. That and the cold stare of those eyes chilled Krow's marrow until he blinked once more, and the panel was just a panel again.

Krow heard a muted buzz and the grating slide of the deadbolts being mechanically drawn back. He waited not a moment but shoved himself inside and slammed the heavy door. After activating the locking sequence on an interior panel, Krow leaned against the back of the door and breathed heavily while the echoes of that sudden entrance galloped along the floors and corridors of the house.

It was crypt-cold inside, and Krow went to the keypad of the thermostat and punched it up a few degrees. Then a few more, just for good measure. He eyed the thermostat suspiciously a moment, but there was no spectral Chastain in its mechanisms. "Bah," Krow said.

He removed his overcoat and flung it over the stair rail. Using his phone's flashlight, rather than turning on the house lights, he began his ascent to the third floor. To say that those three flights of stairs creaked and groaned would be an understatement on the order of calling a hurricane a light breeze. Each step brought a new complaint as if all the stairs, by one accord, had decided they were not fond of the one climbing them.

Krow's chambers on the third floor were nearly as large as an apartment. He opened his door to the main sitting room where the red remnants of an old fire smoldered behind a steel-mesh fireplace screen. The embers emitted a sudden pop, causing Krow to jump.

He sighed, berated himself under his breath, and shut the door behind him. The security panel on the inside wall was very similar to the one by the front door. Krow was not in the habit of locking himself away in his own room, but on this night, he activated every feature. The deadbolts slid into place: one, two, three. The four-inch-square screen indicated that the motion detectors throughout the rest of the house were armed and that all was well.

But Krow was not yet finished, not yet ready to settle in. He had rooms to check. The dining room, bedroom, and library were all as they should be. No one in any of the closets. No one in the darkest alcoves. And no one under the tables or under his bed.

Quite satisfied with his present fortifications, Krow removed his suit coat and went to work on the fire. After a few well-aimed pokes, the embers seemed angry enough, so he tossed on a dry log and replaced the screen. Exhaling deeply, he fell into one of the two armchairs by the hearth and sat for a moment in thoughtless silence.

The embers accepted the new fuel, and licks of flame began

to consume it. Krow, meanwhile, awakened from his trance and poured himself two fingers of Trinidad rum from the dark bottle he kept on the chair-side table. Krow downed the snifter and poured one more finger of the cloudy burnt amber liquid. Then, as meticulous as ever, he dutifully took his bedtime medications. This one for anxiety. That one for depression. And one more just to help him sleep. It was, his psychiatrist promised, not a dangerous combination—these meds and the rum—but would rather create a glorious and restful semi-catatonic night of unbroken sleep. Krow liked it that way: deep and dreamless.

Capping the last of the meds, Krow heard a soft *bing.* Knowing its origin, he turned his head to observe the control panel by his door. In the single column of tiny green lights, the bottom light had gone ominously red. The motion detectors had picked up something moving in the basement.

Krow shook his head. "Bloody rats," he muttered. "Why can't the exterminators do the job once and for all?"

In a moment, the basement light went back to green, and Krow relaxed...prematurely, for the door to the basement crashed open with a sound like a thunderclap, and the next light up, the first floor light, turned to red.

In scrambling for his phone, Krow nearly knocked over his 31-year-old bottle of rum. He needn't have bothered; there was no signal. He tried the emergency app that was supposed to use any nearby wireless network, password protected or not, to send out a 911 to authorities, but the phone shut itself down the moment he opened the app.

Krow dropped his phone at the sound of the chains. Somewhere on the stairs between the first and second floors, there came a great clanking. The first floor light on the control panel went green, and the second floor light turned red. The clanking went on, as if mighty links of chain were being slowly pulled over each individual step. Krow remembered the old stories of ghosts and haunted houses. The ghosts were often illustrated as entities dragging chains.

"Hogwash!" Krow growled.

Ebenezer Krow. The sorrowful moan sounded infinitely distant and yet far too close for Krow's comfort.

"It's nonsense!" Krow muttered, gripping the chair's arms so
fiercely as to turn his knuckles white. "I won't believe it!"

The second floor light went green. The third floor light
turned red, and there came the sounds of clanking and shambling just outside Krow's door.

A jet of pale blue flame erupted at the bottom of the door
and began to spread. It climbed up and over and back down,
completing a perfect outline of the door. The fire burned actively
but made no sound. One by one, the deadbolts drew back. Krow
held his breath. There seemed to be some maniacal hesitation
for a few seconds, and both the fire around the door and the
flames in the fireplace stopped moving.

"GAAAAAHHH!" came a bloodcurdling cry. It came through
the door right before Krow's bulging eyes.

The blue fire leaped from the doorframe and engulfed the
apparition, and Krow's fire roared to life as if to say, "I know
him! Chastain's ghost!" Immediately, that fire died back to a wavering flicker.

Krow found that he could not shut his eyes, nor will himself to leave his chair. He stared at Marley Chastain, the very
same man he'd known for all those years. The very same face:
the large bent nose, the crooked jaw, and those enormous,
half-hooded eyes. Chastain was dressed as if for business or
perhaps for church. He wore a long overcoat, a suit coat, and
suspenders that barely enabled his trousers to linger beneath
his prodigious gut. But for three aspects, this was Chastain as
Krow had always known him. One: Krow found that he could
see through Chastain's body, much as one might see through
a fogged window. Two: the pale blue fire surrounded Chastain,
forming his outline much as it had done the door. And three: he
was indeed bound by chains. These were formidable chains of
cold steel, each link an inch or more thick. It was long and began
twice-wound around Chastain's neck, and then crisscrossed its
way to his black shoes until finally ending like the train of robe

behind him. Krow stared at these chains closely and found that it was connected to—seemingly welded to—a series of old law books, keys, padlocks, clocks (each set to midnight), and legal pads, all of which were wrought in the same steel as the chains.

"You are an intruder here!" Krow managed, summoning his most stinging courtroom tone. "What do you want with me?"

"Much!" It was Chastain's voice that came from those flame-wreathed lips.

"Who are you?"

"You know very well who I am. Ask me *what* I am."

"Well, what are you then?" Krow asked, his ire overtaking his terror. "A ghost?"

"Speak of me as a ghost if it will suffice for you, but a projection is closer to the real. For I am here but not here, residing in another realm of which I am not permitted to speak."

Krow kneaded the armrests with his knuckles. "Spirit, you trouble me standing there," he said. "Can such as you...what I mean to say is, can you, er...sit?"

"I can."

"Well, do it then," Krow said, gesturing toward the second armchair just across from his own. Suddenly aware of the impropriety, he added, "Please."

Chastain dragged his heavy burden and came closer to Krow but ignored the chair. Instead he took a seat on thin air.

This act disturbed Krow greatly, for it was such an otherworldly sight: Chastain, draped in blue flames and heavy chains, in a seated position, hovering two feet off of the floor. "How can you...I'm sorry, I mean, what are you sitting upon?"

"Remember," Chastain warned, and he fixed Krow with a bloodshot eye, "I am a projection. Where I am and what I sit upon...you do not want to know."

Though he thought of several follow up questions, he ignored his legal training and decided to concede the point. He didn't want to know. And he didn't care.

"You don't believe what you see, what you feel, what you hear," Chastain observed.

"I do not," Krow said.

"What other evidence of my reality would the courtroom of your mind accept beyond that of your senses?"

Krow licked his lips. "I...I don't know."

"What cause have you for doubting your senses?"

"Many," said Krow. "So many things can cheat a man's senses. Perhaps, there was something undercooked in my boiled dinner. Or, it could be that I am overworked and fell asleep in this chair. You might be just a dream. Ah, I have it; yes, it's my medication. I wouldn't be the first person to have mysterious and frightening visions on anti-anxiety medications. I'll wager there's more of Prozac than projection about you, whatever you are."

Krow had never been known for his humor, at least not for any sort of good humor. Nor was he feeling smug or clever. He was in fact trying to distract himself from Chastain's ever-staring form. One eye was bad enough, but two were nearly more than Krow could bear. It was the fixed deadness of the eyes, the cataract occlusions, and the ghastly color that shot through Krow to his marrow.

"You see this?" Krow said, grabbing up one of his pill bottles.

"I do," the spirit replied.

Krow frowned. "But you're staring at me."

"Nonetheless, I see it."

"Well, then!" Krow volleyed back. "I have but to swallow just a meager handful of these blue pills and be chased and chastised by ghouls, ghosts, and hobgoblins—all of my own making. Hogwash, I tell you! You are nothing but HOGWASH!"

"GAAAAAHHH!" Chastain shrieked, shaking his chains and its accoutrements with such perilous vigor that Krow felt faint. The blue flames around the spirit writhed as if kindled by Chastain's virulent ire. Krow slid from his chair, dropped to his knees, and raised his hands with plaintive trembling.

"Have mercy!" Krow pleaded. "Dire phantom, why do you return to your old abode? Why trouble me?"

"Man of the legal mind!" replied the ghost. "Do you believe in me or not?"

"I...I do," Krow said. "I have no choice! But why would a spirit like you appear once more on earth? Why appear to me?"

"It is required of every soul," the ghost replied, "to see in vivid likeness all the world and its fellows, far and wide; and if that soul denies the blessed gift in life, it is condemned to recall all that might have been if it had been...otherwise! Oh, woe is me! What love I could have had, what love I could have shared by the mercy He offered! But I refused!"

Again, the apparition shrieked and whipped its chains about and dug its nails into its sallow cheeks, leaving trails like raw but spoiled meat.

"There are flames around you," Krow said, his voice tremulous. "Tell me why?"

At this the spirit turned its head and raised one hand to watch the blue licks of fire dance upon its fingers. "Always burning," Chastain moaned. "Forever burning and yet...so cold."

"Cold?" Krow blurted, swallowing deeply. "And the chains, the irons...what of those?"

"I wear the evidence of that which I held sacred in life, forging the chain needed to bear it all," the ghost replied. "I crafted it link by link and yard by yard; I wound it about myself of my own free will and carried it with me, day after wasted day. Do the chain and its elements look unfamiliar to *you*?"

Krow shook violently. His gut twisted like a nest of adders.

"Or would you learn," continued the spirit, "the form and weight of the unbreakable coil you bear yourself? It was as grim and heavy as this, seven Christmas Eves past. You have labored lustily on it since. It is a burdensome, unwieldy chain!"

Krow obeyed the urge to search about himself, expecting to find miles of chain surrounding him, but could see nothing.

"Marley," Krow implored. "Good old Marley Chastain, reveal more of this mystery to me. Comfort me."

"Comfort?" the spirit echoed. "Comfort is the last thing you need, and discomfort is what I have come to bring. Oh, that I paid heed to the discomforts of life when they paid me such blessed visits! They were the wounds of a friend and dearly bought. But

I ignored them. My spirit was poisoned by precedent, vivisected by ambition, and finally cremated by convictions ignored. Cases won with guile and conceit, manufactured evidence, and bewildering court histrionics. Woe!"

"But, Marley, you were always a good man of law."

"Law!" cried the ghost. "Alas! Love should have been my law. Understanding, tenderness, forgiveness, friendship, and the good of my fellow man—all should have been my law! The dealings of our firm were but a grain of filth in the comprehensive fertile soil of what should have been my law!"

Chastain opened his mouth but this time in a silent scream, and he shook his chains such that they battered his revenant body. Then, his arms fell to his sides. "Of all the times of your calendar year," the spirit continued, "I feel anguish most keenly at Christmas. Why did I walk through and past crowds of those in need with my nose buried in a book? Had I but looked up, might I have been aware of the blessed star which led the wise men to a singularly poor lodging? Would not the light of that star have led me to others of the poor and downtrodden? Not poor in money only, but poor in spirit? GAAAAAHHH!"

Krow ducked his head and stared into the fire behind the screen.

In a dreadfully quiet voice, Chastain said, "Weary days without number await me."

Krow wrung his hands. "Is...is there no hope for you, then?"

"For me?" the ghost returned. "No. I personally nailed shut the door of redemption long ago and rejoiced at the searing of my soul. Now, all is darkness. All is cold. And there is gnashing of teeth. I have come for your sake, Ebenezer. There is yet a child's chance of your reclamation."

"You were always a true friend, Marley," said Krow. "Thank you."

"Tonight, you will be haunted by three messengers."

Tears flooded Krow's eyes. "Is...is this prolonged haunting the chance you spoke of, Marley?"

"It is."

"I...I'd rather not," said Krow.

"Without the gravity of their appearance," said the ghost, "you have no hope but to follow in my misbegotten footsteps. Expect the first when the bell tolls one."

"Couldn't they all come at once? Now?" Krow asked. "And get it over with?"

"Expect the second upon the stroke of two. The third will come when the chime of three ceases its resonance. And beware, Ebenezer, for of these three, one is a miscreant come from my eternal dwelling and bears you nothing but malice."

"Which one?" Krow demanded. "First, second, or third?"

"I know not," answered the specter. "And I fear for your sake that you have not the eyes to see nor ears to hear. Turn away from me now, Ebenezer Krow, for the time of our parting is at hand. But watch that you remember what has transpired here tonight."

Krow turned away as he'd been told. At first. But at the labored shambling of his dead partner's feet, he could not keep his eyes downcast. He watched as the blue flames leaped from Chastain and carved an irregular hollow into the floor. There darkness boiled. The spirit's chains unraveled somewhat and several coils escaped into the shuddering darkness of that hole and went taut. Chastain resisted their pull to no avail and was slowly, relentlessly drawn down into the pit.

Out of some desperate form of curiosity, Krow followed to the spot and peered over the edge. A stair of blue fire spiraled down into the unknown distance, and Chastain was already far away.

Something flashed up from the darkness. Something like teeth and fire and an eye. The floor returned like the slamming of a trapdoor. And Krow skittered backward as fast as he could crawl.

He saw the control panel by his door. Every light was green. The deadbolts were thrown. His sitting room was just as it had always been. Krow stood up, brushed himself off, and glanced at his bottle of rum. He turned away from it and started to say, "Hogwash," but thought the first syllable might be more than enough.

He found himself more weary than he could ever remember feeling and went straight to bed. He shut his bedroom door but did not undress. Instead, he fell into his bed, buried himself beneath the blankets, and went instantly to sleep.

STAVE II

THE FIRST OF THE THREE SPIRITS

WHEN KROW AWOKE, was so dark that looking through his mesh bed curtains revealed naught but a murky world with no distinguishing features. He knew by habit where the dresser was, the closet too, and the roll top desk Chastain had left behind. He knew, of course, where the library and sitting room doors were and where the single arched window should be—but he couldn't see them. Still, he diligently tried to pierce the gloom with his weasel's eyes. In that effort, Krow was sorely frustrated and then immediately made anxious by the single toll of the heavy bell of St. Marie a few blocks away.

Frantically, he cast about for his phone, and, in failing, realized hopelessly that he'd left it in the sitting room on the chair side table. Then, the whole of Chastain's ghostly visit came crashing into his consciousness.

Even as the toll's last resonance began to fade, Krow remembered Chastain's words: "Expect the first when the bell tolls one."

"One," he muttered. "One o'clock in the morning. What—"

The words died and decayed on his lips when he became aware of a gray presence moving right to left from the window side of the chamber, past the closet door and the dresser, and then turning toward the bed.

Krow bashed himself nearly senseless on his headboard as the hooded thing drew near and its eyes appeared, burning like white flame. A hand—I am telling you, a fiercely glowing hand—pulled aside the bed curtain. And Krow found himself face-to-hood with this supernatural visitor; as close to it as I am to you now. For though you may not feel it, I am standing in the spirit right beside you.

"Are you the messenger?" Krow whispered. "The one whose arrival was predicted to me?"

"I am." The voice that answered was uncannily difficult to discern, for it seemed both male and female, both tender as sunshine and hard as flint.

Krow found with dismay that he could not push himself any further back, for the headboard was snugly fixed to the wall. "Who are you?" Krow asked. "Or what are you?"

The hooded figure straightened up, and its robes shifted, revealing several blinding glimpses of light. "What difference does it make what I am?" the androgynous voice replied, a keen edge to each word. "Ghost, spirit, apparition, messenger, specter, or wraith? No matter which one you choose, you will be in most ways...wrong."

"But I am a man of law," Krow said. "Terms are critical to my endeavors."

"Then, choose."

"I am," Krow stammered. "Er, I have. You seem more ghostly than anything else."

"Done!" the visitor called out, as if sealing a bargain. "Therefore, I am the Ghost of Christmas Past!" With that pronouncement, the spirit disrobed. Incandescent white light flooded the bedroom.

Krow covered his face with both arms and cringed.

"Look upon me," said the ghost.

"I...I cannot," Krow replied. "Or I'll be blinded."

"Whether you have ever not been so is very much in debate," the ghost replied. "But very well, I shall dampen my power. Look upon me, man."

The flaring, painful light died away, and Krow put down his arms. Before him stood a tall figure garbed in a combination of white linen and silver armor. There was a heavy sword girt at the ghost's side. Indeed, it appeared to Krow as a Valkyrie from Norse mythology brought to life. But, there was no tell-tale sign of the ghost being woman or man. Long blonde hair was contained by a gleaming silver circlet. It had high, arching brows over slightly canted but overly large, clear gray eyes. Its nose was prominent but not oversized for its face. A grim expression formed upon the ghost's full lips, and its square jaw was set and rigid.

The ghost seemed much more solid than Chastain's form had been. Krow could not see through him...or her. And, while its brilliance had indeed been toned down, it kindled now and again in places as if threatening to return to its sun-like radiance.

"What would one like you, bright as a morning star, want with a creature like me?" Krow asked.

"I have come for your welfare," the ghost replied. It put out its hand and took hold of Krow's forearm with an iron grip. "Rise and travel with me."

Krow felt powerless to resist and slid from the bed, but upon seeing that their path led toward the room's lone window, he cried out, "I am just human. I cannot fly. And...and I need my cane!"

"Bearing my touch, and in my company," said the ghost, "you will tread where eagles dare and beyond."

Krow felt no pain in his hip. In a blink, he felt no weight at all, as if he'd been suspended above the ground. But his room was gone. Manchester was gone, leaving no trace of that old New England city. For a moment, there was naught but wheeling stars and blurring landscapes. Darkness took all of that as well, and Krow looked about for some point of reference to stay his nauseating dizziness. A vision appeared in his periphery. It was blurry and wavering, like looking at one's reflection in moving water. Krow realized with astonishment that he was looking at an undulating mirror image of himself and the ghost. Perhaps, it was a trick of the movement, but there were details in the image that Krow, try as he might, could not reconcile. The image of himself seemed to be smiling broadly as if on a joyride of some kind. *That is definitely wrong*, thought Krow. *I haven't smiled in... well, in a very long time.*

The spirit's mirror image too had unusual features. It was still uncannily bright, but flickered much like lightning beneath a stormy mantle. And Krow couldn't see the spirit's eyes, only quivering sockets of darkness.

"Spirit!" Krow exclaimed. "What is this I see as we travel? Some kind of reflection?"

The ghost kept its eyes fixed straight ahead, and its hold on Krow's forearm tightened somewhat. "Where we journey," said the ghost, "there are other travelers on other errands. You may call this a reflection, for now."

When Krow again felt something beneath his feet, he looked down and saw sand. He also noted that he was now dressed in his least favorite bedtime robe and a pair of bed slippers. The moon was so bright and the stars so distinct, Krow thought he should feel cold, but he felt quite the opposite. Primitive white buildings rose up all around, and there were palm trees spread intermittently across what appeared to be a large courtyard. A large crowded courtyard.

"Spirit," said Krow, "I do not know this place."

"No?" echoed the ghost. "Perhaps a closer view will remind you."

The spirit led Krow by the arm into the crowd, moving people aside with each step.

"Excuse us!" Krow blurted.

"They cannot hear you," the ghost said. "Nor can they see you."

"But clearly, they feel us, for you keep pushing them aside."

"What they feel is no more than a breath of wind or the sudden compulsion to shrink to one side or the other. Our presence here will not be recognized in any regard."

The spirit led Krow deeper and deeper into the crowd and to the threshold of a broad open hall. People pressed to get inside, and many stood upon tip-toe all along the outside wall to get a glimpse inside a window.

"In here?" Krow asked.

The ghost nodded and led him inside. Through the door, they were greeted by warm flickering firelight from ensconced torches, as well as a fire in a grated stone hearth in the center of the room. There were great platters of food set about: steaming bread, dried fish, piles of olives and dates, pomegranates, figs, and grapes.

The most motley gathering of people Krow had ever seen filled the room; some standing, some reclining by low tables and enjoying the sumptuous feast. Those standing on the room's perimeter were mostly men, dressed resplendently in striped tunics and robes. Most wore a kind of heavy shawl over their shoulders and over some kind of headdress or turban. And dangling from their sleeves, their sashes, and their robes were all manner of glimmering tassels and strange ornamental boxes. Many of these decorated men were busy shouting at others, especially the swarthy men busily slurping from cups and licking their fingers. Krow could see the indignant fury written on the faces of the elites but couldn't understand their angry words.

The chamber contained a fair number of women also, breathtakingly beautiful women. Their eyes were tawny brown or jade green and ever so striking, set within dark lashes and brows and surrounded by smooth tan skin. All but their faces, hands, and feet were covered, but their robes and tunics were cinched with ornate belts that emphasized shapes and curves. Some of these women had bracelets, anklets, earrings, and nose jewels. Krow couldn't help but stare. In his eyes, many of these women had a promiscuous way about them, constantly touching the men in their presence. Krow thought he'd caught the eye of one of the sensual women, blushed brilliantly, and turned away—

only to remind himself that these people could not see him.

While some in the room were preoccupied with their own endeavors and conversations, the majority of the chamber directed their attention to a single man seated by the chamber's back wall. He too wore robes and coverings but nothing ornate. He too had darkly tanned skin, his differing only in the reddish tint on his cheekbones. His hair was dark and draped back over his broad shoulders. His eyes were large and brown, gleaming in the firelight, and he wore a fuzzy beard that swayed upon his chest as he spoke.

"I'm sorry," Krow said, "but I cannot understand this man's speech. I don't know this language."

The ghost sighed and tightened his grip on Krow's arm. Instantly, Krow began to understand what the man and those around him were saying.

"...am grateful, Matthew, for your company and for all you have provided."

"It is not often that a rabbi would share a meal in the home of a tax collector. You are different, Jesus."

Krow went rigid and backed toward the door, but the ghost barred his way.

"Spirit," Krow stammered, "just how...how far back is this Christmas past?"

Hand on the hilt of its sword, the ghost replied, "Open your eyes. What does the evidence tell you? This is a Christmas long before Christmas came to be all that you abhor."

Krow pointed a shaky finger. "Is he who I think he is?" The ghost nodded.

Just then, one of the tantalizingly beautiful women knelt by Jesus and delicately caressed his jawline down to his chin.

"How dare she!" Krow shouted.

The ghost snorted and said, "Remember, they cannot hear you."

Jesus took hold of the woman's hand, enclosing it tenderly in both of his own. For what seemed an eternity to Krow, Jesus and this woman stared deeply at each other. Then, tears began to cascade down her cheeks. She suddenly drew back her hand and bowed her head.

Jesus reached over, gently lifted her chin, and said, "Go in peace. You no longer have anything to fear from Heaven or man."

"Blasphemy!" came a chorus of spitting mad shouts from the room's periphery.

One of the immaculately dressed men cried out, "He calls himself rabbi but dines with prostitutes and tax collectors!"

"He breaks bread with sinners!" screamed another man.

Jesus looked up and sent a piercing glare around the chamber. "It is not the healthy who need a physician, but rather the sick. But go and learn what this means: I desire mercy, not sacrifice. For I have not come to call the righteous, but sinners."

"Learn?" a many-tasseled, gray-bearded man blurted. "You dare tell us to learn? You who are just thirty or so years in this world? You go ahead and keep company with your sinner friends. We will travel and dine elsewhere."

"What do you think?" asked the ghost. "These men have somewhat of a point, do they not?"

Krow couldn't take his eyes off of Jesus. "I...I do not know what to say."

"You don't?" The spirit raised an ethereal eyebrow. "But you were so sure at the Bleak House Tavern, were you not?"

Krow said nothing.

"Stop!" Jesus said, and the ornately robed men turned. "Woe to you, teachers of the law and Pharisees, you hypocrites! You travel over land and sea to win a single convert, and when you have succeeded, you make them twice as much a child of hell as you are."

This infuriated the departing men all the more. They screamed and cried out, some of them tearing at their own robes. When the tumult had ended, the chamber was empty but for the "sinners" and Jesus.

Krow said, "Spirit, I think I ought to leave as well. Take me from this place."

"One moment more," the ghost replied, pointing.

Krow watched Jesus take up a leather bag and pour wine from it into Matthew's cup.

"This isn't real," Krow grumbled, shoving his way toward the exit. "This isn't the Jesus I know."

The ghost put his hands on Krow's shoulders. "This is the only Jesus. Are you certain you can stomach being associated with Him?"

"Take me away from this"—Krow started to say "illusion" but thought better of it—"place."

"Perhaps a journey to something and someone more familiar," the ghost said, pushing Krow through the door.

When Krow emerged on the other side, he found himself in a whitened country landscape with delicate gossamer flakes still falling. They stood at the top of a hill and, as they watched, several youths in dull plaid uniforms and overstuffed downy coats came running by and, leaping upon their sleds, went careening down the slope.

"Heavens!" Krow said. "I know this place. This is Scully's Hill in Bartlett...in the White Mountains! I attended parochial school here. So...so long ago."

"You are shaking," remarked the ghost.

"It's the cold," Krow said, hugging himself and then wiping at his eyes. "Bitter cold here this time of year, but, on the other hand, Scully's Hill was the best place for sledding for miles..." His voice trailed off as a few of the youngsters, clambering back up the hill, came into view.

"No," Krow said, "it cannot be. That's Neil Bains! And that girl there, Barbara McKinley. My word! Ha, ha! We had to wear those old uniforms, but Barbara had every pink accessory known to human kind! And...I'd know that fellow anywhere. That's Antonio Jackson. So smooth and cool, and yet, he chose to let me be his friend. We were best friends. This is...this is when we were nine, maybe ten years old!"

As the youths approached, Krow couldn't help himself. He cried out, "Hello, Neil! Hello, Barbara! I see you've still got that old Flexible Flyer with the rails painted pink! Ha, ha! And, Antonio! I've missed you, lad. How—"

"They cannot hear you," the ghost said, irritation grating in his words. "These are the echoes of things that have been."

Krow crossed his arms and scowled. A momentary imp of the perverse took his thoughts and he was genuinely tempted to grab Antonio's sled and go whooshing down the hill himself. But a somber note came that quelled the enthusiasm instantly and he said, "I never had a friend as true as Antonio, not before or after. I don't remember what caused us to part, but now, I recently heard he was killed in a home invasion."

"It is a marvel, is it not?" the ghost probed.

"What?"

"A young African American boy, such profound friends... with you."

"It was," Krow conceded. "My father never knew, really. Our friendship kindled at school, and I couldn't bring him to my home. My father was a rather old-fashioned man."

"You mean a prejudiced man, don't you?" inquired the spirit.

Krow stared down at the snow. "Yes, that's a rather acidic term these days but all too true." Krow shook his head slowly.

"What is it?"

"Nothing."

"Are you certain?"

"Yes, well...no," Krow stammered. "I mean, there were two people, a man and a woman, who paid me a visit just this evening. They were collecting donations to help the poor, especially children. I sent them away. Seeing myself—all of us, really—as children, well, I would like to have given them something, that's all."

Just then, another young man with a sled came sprinting into the scene. He gave Antonio a playful push and raced down the hill.

"Oh, no you don't, Ebenezer!" Antonio cried. "No one beats me on this hill. I own this hill!" And just like that, Antonio was off, and the two boys raced side by side to the bottom.

"Who won?" asked the ghost.

"I...I think I did," Krow replied. "I had a head start, but, uh, I think Antonio let me win."

Krow watched his younger self and Antonio come leaping up the slope, bantering and laughing the whole way. At the top, they readied their sleds and counted aloud, "1...2..."

At three, another child supplanted himself in front of the sledders. Krow recognized the red-haired lad immediately. It was Clarence Abernathy, and he said, "Ebenezer, you need to go back."

"What? Why?" asked the young Krow.

"Rector Levesque said so," Clarence replied. "Your Latin scores are still too low, and you're to have private tutoring this afternoon."

At this, the elder Krow stiffened. His jaw went slack, and his eyes grew almost to match old Chastain's huge lamps.

"I forgot all about that," the young Krow said. "But it's the best snowfall this winter. Tell the Rector we'll meet another day."

"You tell him," Clarence said, brusquely turning his back to Krow and walking intently toward an unoccupied sled.

"Don't go, Ebenezer," Antonio pleaded. "We're just getting started. That old buzz saw can wait."

The young Krow stared at the ground. "If I don't go, it will just make things worse."

Antonio looked up knowingly, anger kindling on his brow. "Will he...will he hurt you again?"

"Antonio," Krow said, "I told you not to talk about that. Please!"

"He'd better not," Antonio whispered. "He'd better not."

The young Krow gave Antonio a broken smile and then turned to trudge back to the rectory.

"We will follow him," said the ghost.

"No, please, no!" Krow cried out, his deeper older voice sounding remarkably like his nine-year-old self. He tried to twist out of the spirit's grip, but he'd have had a better chance escaping a bear trap.

"Come along, Ebenezer," the spirit said. "Our journey is far from over."

They followed the younger Krow's footprints in the snow. They watched as he approached the chapel and disappeared within.

The elder Krow stared up at the building. The chapel was very old, even then, but beautiful in its aging grace. There were three large stained glass window panels. Krow didn't need to see them again to know what they depicted, but he looked anyway.

The first panel, all deep purples, blues, browns, and soaring whites, showed Abraham standing on a hill, gazing up at the night sky. The translucent hand of God was upon the patriarch's shoulder as He promised Abraham offspring numbering as the stars.

The second panel was Jesus sitting beneath a tree with a lap full of children, the disciples nearby looking like they'd been baptized in vinegar.

The third panel struck Krow now more than it ever had when he was a youth. It was Jesus standing upon a precipice with a dark figure standing behind him, pointing off toward a distant horizon.

The spirit gave Krow a shove and pointed ahead. "In there," he said.

Krow looked back as if there might be some chance of escape, but there was none. He slowly approached the chapel, noting the beautiful snow cover all along the roof. But at the rectory, the snow stopped. The shingled roof was blackened as if by smoke. Whatever insulation might have been in the upper confines of that building, it was not enough to contain the heat within. The snow had no chance.

Krow entered by the chapel's side door. They walked in silence by the pews. Krow did not glance back at the stained glass or the altar. He stared straight ahead at the path: the threadbare carpet, the stains in the corners, the cobwebs dressing the vestibule like gossamer garlands.

Krow saw his younger self, yes, he did. He saw him rap upon that dark door at the end of the hall. He saw his younger self bathed in sickly yellow light as the door opened. And he wept uncontrollably as his younger self entered Rector Levesque's private study.

"We must follow," the ghost said.

Krow fell to his knees. "Please, Spirit, I beg of you. Do not make me do this. Do not let me see. Is not the memory seared into my mind forever already?"

"Tell me, Christian man," said the ghost, "why are you repelled by most Christians? Is it not because they deserve to be repelled? Is it not because they are more repugnant and broken than those they single out as...sinners?"

Krow's lips moved restlessly, but no words emerged. He stared into the spirit's emotionless gray eyes.

"Coward," the spirit muttered, yanking Krow to his feet and dragging him toward the door.

"Spirit," Krow pleaded, "why are you saying this? Why do you seem to rejoice in my misery?"

"Stand up, worldly man," the ghost said, its voice dropping an octave. "Face your past. Face the truth."

The ghost shoved Krow at the door. Krow's entire body trembled, but it was an uncanny kind of movement, a very, very tight vibration, something from so deep inside the man that his entire being went into distress.

"Open the door," the spirit commanded.

Krow could scarcely breathe. He released a strange breath, a piercing wheeze, and turned the glass knob.

He fell, eyes closed, into the room with a worse haunt than any spirit he had thus far met screaming out its marrow-freezing wail of remembrance in his tortured mind.

When Krow opened his eyes again, he saw that the door had not opened into Rector Levesque's study at all. He'd fallen flat on his face on the floor of some kind of vast open building.

"Do you know this place?" asked the ghost.

Krow stood and found he was in a warehouse that had been converted into a series of offices. Every office, cubicle, and library had been decorated with pine and holly, festive garlands, and sparkling colored lights. And these offices were bustling with workers, bustling with the greatest fervor a business could ever hope for.

"Do I know this place?" a transformed Krow echoed. "This is Old Fezziwick's law office. I was a clerk here for seven years."

Just then, a distant bell tolled once, twice, and all the way to seven. The busy hum of the building stopped immediately. Heads popped up out of cubicles, and everyone stared at the library elevated upon a platform at the front of the vast hall. From behind one of the dozens of ten-foot-tall bookcases, strode a portly man, carrying a massive open book. I tell you, this tome weighed forty pounds if it weighed an ounce!

The man wore long gray hair, tastefully pulled back in a tail, sideburns down to his round jaw, and a stern expression that looked quite absurd given his red and green suit and the colorful lights blinking Christmas cheer from a novelty necklace. He came precariously close to the edge of the platform, and with mighty force, slammed the immense book shut. The sound echoed like a cannon shot, and everyone in warehouse cheered.

"Who would believe it?" asked Krow as he moved toward the front. "Old Fezziwick, alive again!"

"That's enough work for today!" Fezziwick cried out, his cheeks full of jovial blush. "In fact, that's enough work for today, tomorrow, and the day after that. It's Christmas Eve, and our company party awaits!"

Employees in nearly every office flew into action, working in teams to carry away a half dozen extraordinarily long tables and an army of chairs.

Fezziwick bounded down the stairs and shouted, "Birds! Birds, where are you? I thought I made it clear, no more work!"

Krow turned and looked at one particular cubicle. Two heads popped up. His own, but as a young man in his mid-twenties. The other, a narrow-faced gentleman with a shining cap of black hair, raised his arms as if surrendering and called out, "Very sorry, Mr. Fezziwick. Bird One, reporting for party preparations!"

The younger Krow responded in kind, "Bird Two, ready for festivities!"

"That's Drew Dovel," the elder Krow explained, turning to the ghost. "A jewel of a young man, if ever there was one. A hard worker, too."

"But you didn't always get along so well," the ghost said.

"Not always," Krow replied. "He was so heavily invested in the whole 'Born Again Christian' movement. It sometimes impacted his work."

The ghost tilted his head. "How so?"

"Well, he gravitated toward civil rights issues and all too often poured himself into pro bono work, leaving paying clients underserved."

"There you are, my Bird Boys," Fezziwick said. "Drew, why don't you head to the landing, eh? I'm sure the caterers could use a hand or two. Ebenezer, meet me in my office."

"Old Fezziwick took to calling us his 'Bird Boys,'" Krow explained over his shoulder, following his younger self to a room enclosed by smoky glass. "It was due, of course, to our names. But he always used to say of us, 'Sharp of eye and ready to fly.' That meant a lot to me, then."

The office door closed, but the ghost and Krow passed through its thin walls as if they were a curtain of rain. On the other side, Fezziwick sat in a high, leather-backed chair that swiveled. He was reaching behind the chair and talking a mile a minute.

"...Positively ecstatic about the gift I've found for your partner in crime," he said. "And you know how hard Drew is to shop for."

"Truly," the twenty-something Krow replied. "He told me not to get him anything at all this year, but rather to donate what I might have spent."

"Ha, ha!" Fezziwick laughed. "He told me the same thing, but I'll do him one better. I've found the perfect thing." He turned and handed Krow a book with a red and gold dustcover.

"*Strength to Love*," Krow said, "by Dr. Martin Luther King Jr."

"What do you think, Ebenezer? Perfect, is it not?"

Krow nodded and gave a sideways sort of smile. "It is the perfect gift for Drew. I'm sure he'll cherish it."

"Ha, ha! That's just what I thought. It just came out, you know, but I had an advanced copy and read it cover-to-cover in a weekend. It's truly amazing work. Do you know, Dr. King said something in this book that I just cannot shake. He said, 'Darkness cannot drive out darkness, only light can do that. Hate cannot drive out hate, only love can do that.' In our day and time, especially at Christmas, I feel my own heart resonating with those words. Don't you, Ebenezer?"

"To a degree," Krow replied.

"To a great degree tonight, I hope," Fezziwick said. "I'll wrap this in a jiffy and be right out. And don't you worry, Ebenezer, there'll be a gift beneath the tree for you, too. Now, won't you join Drew and help the caterers get set up? We have a hungry brood here to feed!"

The elder Krow and his haunting companion exited the office and observed as the Fezziwick Law Office was transformed into a Christmas ballroom.

Streamers and more lights were hung, as well as mistletoe in strategic locations. The Bird Boys came careening in with a platoon of caterers. There was a gigantic steamship round roast, several turkeys bursting with stuffing, heaping mountains of buttered green beans, potatoes—baked, mashed, and boiled— enough for fifty people to eat nothing but and be positively stuffed with an equal amount leftover!

There were great hams, vats of macaroni and cheese, broccoli and cheese, and any other casserole that might be produced with massive quantities of cheese.

The desserts too were magnificent: mince pies, pumpkin pies, pecan pies, extraordinary triple layer cakes, angel-food cakes, and shortcakes. These were surrounded by at least thirty varieties of Christmas cookies and a circle of jovial gingerbread men.

The caterers wheeled in seven kegs of beer, several dozen cases of wine, and a vast assortment of other spirits to boot. The band arrived and set up in no time. And then came the guests.

Mrs. Fezziwick came in like a comet, dressed in a dazzling red Christmas gown. By that point, Mr. Fezziwick had emerged and, at the sight of his stunning wife, slapped his hand upon his breast feigning a heart attack.

The elder Krow clapped his hands and bounced where he stood. "I remember this night so vividly now," he told the spirit. "Funny, I haven't thought of it for so long."

"That is not all you haven't thought of for many long years."

Just then, streaming out of the throng entering the ballroom, came two young ladies. One of them, a cherubic beauty with curly red hair and constellations of freckles, nearly tackled the younger Krow.

"Fran!" he exclaimed.

"Fran!" the elder Krow exclaimed.

"Dear brother," she replied, hugging him thrice more and then peppering his cheeks with affectionate pecks.

"I wasn't sure you'd be able to come," Krow said. "It's so good to see you."

"I know you worried that Father wouldn't allow it, but Ebenezer, he has changed. He's so much gentler and kinder. I believe retirement has given him a new lease on life. We shall go together and visit him for Christmas, and you'll see."

"Your sister," remarked the ghost. "A delicate flower of a woman. She died young."

"Yes," the elder Krow replied. "Too young. They said it was her heart, but it was that good-for-nothing husband of hers that pushed her to despair."

"Difficult to forgive such an offense," the ghost suggested.

"Difficult?" Krow echoed, throwing his shoulders back. "If his alcoholism didn't kill him first, I might have heartily considered it."

"Fran had a child, I think?" the spirit said.

"Yes, my nephew, Fred Bithywell," he replied. "Ah...seeing Fran now, I am reminded of how much Fred looks like his mother...my sister." He turned back to the party.

"And brother," Fran bubbled to the young Krow. "I have brought you the best Christmas present ever: the opportunity to meet my precious friend, Annabelle Prentice."

Young Fran stepped to the side, revealing a raven-haired beauty whose dark eyes framed by long lashes might have been scandalous if not for the demure manner in which she used them.

Krow, young and old alike, stood still and silent, mouths agape and cheeks, ruddy.

"Well, brother," said Fran, "aren't you going to say anything?"

The young Krow looked lost for a moment, but managed to blurt out, "Thank you." His eyes grew wide at the impropriety. "I mean thank you for introducing us," he stammered. "Not that you, Miss Prentice, are a piece of property to be given or received. You are obviously a woman of free will and can do as you please, but...ah, hello."

"Hello, Ebenezer," Annabelle replied. "Fran has told me so much about you."

The voice coming from those tiny plum lips was surprisingly deep, and the sum total of her presence did its work upon young Krow. "Fran tells me you're quite a dancer."

As if on cue, the band struck up a merry melody.

"Oh, I love 'Jingle Bell Rock'," she said, ducking her head a little.

Young Krow took a few seconds more to get the message. "Oh," he said finally, "would you like to dance?"

"I thought you'd never ask." Annabelle offered her hand, and oh, did Krow take it. With Fran clapping enthusiastically, he whisked Annabelle onto the dance floor.

Grinning like an idiot, the elder Krow watched his younger self whirl and twirl Annabelle all about the floor, gaining more and more appreciative spectators as their dance went on.

Drew Dovel took Fran's hand and led her Jingle Bell Rocking right next to her brother, and the four of them worked up such a sweat from their movements that, after the third song, they simply had to stop for a drink of cold punch.

During the whole of this time, old Krow looked on, but he

was not still. Oblivious to the ghost, he acted as if he'd lost his mind, mimicking his younger self's dancing and dreamily mumbling to himself.

It wasn't until Fezziwick's party came to an end that Krow became once more aware of his spectral shepherd. The spirit's eyes seemed ablaze, and Krow felt them boring into him. "What?" he complained. "I was quite an accomplished dancer, once upon a time. When properly motivated, that is."

"A trivial matter," said the ghost, "to provide an atmosphere in which silly people might behave sillier still."

"Trivial?" Krow blurted.

The ghost pointed back to the scene. Young Krow and Drew Dovel were stumbling all over themselves to thank Fezziwick for what they called, "The grandest party that has ever been or ever shall be."

"What else can it be?" asked the ghost. "The man spent a few hundred dollars of your mortal money. Is it such a sum as to deserve all that praise?"

"It's not about the money," Krow grumbled. "Fezziwick had a way about him. With a look or a touch on the shoulder, he had the power encourage the entire office. He made even the most toilsome tasks seem worthwhile and fruitful. The happiness that he bestowed upon us all, well, it was quite a bit more valuable than piles of gold! Why, he—"

Krow felt that blazing glare once more and stopped.

"What is it, mortal man?" asked the ghost.

Krow sighed. "Never you mind," he said. "It's nothing."

"I *do* mind," the ghost insisted, "and I think there *is* something."

Krow paced a small circle. "No," he said, "no, it's just that I wish I could speak to my personal clerk. There are a few things I would like to tell him, that's all."

"My time now grows very short," said the ghost. "Ride the wind!"

Darkness came rushing in with a howling shriek, and Krow once more saw strange blurred images in the distance. But it all cleared away, and Krow saw himself again in the flesh. He was older, in the prime of his life, and he was hurrying across a little bridge to meet a woman on the other side.

"Goodness," Annabelle said, "I was afraid you weren't coming."

"Weren't coming?" he replied as if the very thought was felonious crime. "I had...errands...to run, but I wouldn't miss seeing you on our anniversary."

Annabelle blushed and smiled, but it seemed to the older Krow that her smile was a bit off, perhaps, overly cautious and pensive.

"Do you know why I asked you to meet here?" the young Krow asked, leading her to a seat on the bench.

"Of course," she replied. "This is where we had our first kiss. The snow was falling, and you were so gentle. I was quite surprised by that kiss."

"Well, it seems we've come full circle," Krow said. He had remained standing. "For, today, on our seventh anniversary, I have brought you here again...to surprise you...again."

Krow fell to one knee and immediately removed something from his dark coat's pocket. Annabelle, upon seeing this action and recognizing its portent, became immediately flustered, first with ecstatic joy and then with something more like anxiety.

"From the day we met," Krow began, holding up a diamond ring, "I have known that you are the only woman in this world I would spend a lifetime with. Your beauty caught me, but your kindness kept me. Compared to the immaterial gifts you've given me over the years, I have little to offer, but my heart. Annabelle Prentice, will you—"

"Wait!" she exclaimed. Within one heart's beat, she began to weep so fiercely that the tears leaped off of her cheeks.

"What?" Krow croaked. "Are you saying no?"

"No, it's not that," Annabelle returned.

Krow's rigidity softened, and he held out the ring again.

"I am not saying no, Ebenezer," she cried. "I am only saying wait. Oh, horrid, horrid timing!"

"Have I done something wrong?"

"No, dear Ebenezer," she said, putting her delicate hand to his cheek, "but it cannot wait any longer."

"Spirit," the elder Krow pleaded, "take me from this time. I lived through this. I have no need to see it again."

At this, the ghost's eyes kindled like a flare of golden fire. There came a resonant metallic ring, and before Krow could comprehend what had happened, the ghost's sword was unsheathed at last, its wicked point at Krow's throat.

"Do you know this blade?" the ghost asked, its voice deepening with menace.

"N-no! I've never seen it before!" Krow exclaimed.

"Liar! You have wielded this weapon before. How often you have used it to vanquish others. How often you have slashed it about with impunity, never once recognizing that this is a two-edged sword. Its...blade...cuts...both...ways. Turn and look!"

Krow saw his younger self rise from the kneeling position, standing now so tall that he cast a dusky shadow upon Annabelle, who seemed to be shrinking even as she spoke.

"Do you recall the conversation we had?" she asked. The tears made bloody black rivulets of mascara down her cheeks. "A year after we met, we spoke of very serious matters, dating exclusively, a possible future together—among other things."

The younger Krow no longer held out the ring. He had it clenched in his fist at his side. "I remember," he said, his voice void of spirit.

Annabelle sighed, looked left and right, as if searching for but failing to find a route of escape. "That night, Ebenezer, you confided in me that you had never been with another woman, that, according to the Scriptures, you would remain celibate until...until marriage."

"Where are you going with this?"

"Please, try and understand," she said. "I was unprepared. I had no idea you were so serious. You were staring at me then, just like you are now. You were beckoning for a response...and I gave you one. I was so afraid. I didn't know what to say, so I told you that I too was saving myself for marriage. That much was true, but...but I told you I had never been with a man."

Krow coughed out the words, "You... you mean... you lied?"

"I panicked!" she cried. "I thought if I told you, you would leave me."

"And you would have been right!" Krow's face contorted, sorrow and rage struggling for supremacy. "All this time? We've been together all this time, and you've never thought to tell me?"

"A thousand times I thought to tell you!" Her entire body shuddered. "But I didn't know how."

"Well, waiting until I propose is certainly not the right way!" Krow shoved the ring into his coat pocket and threw his hands up in the air. "All this time, I saw you as the purest blossom, but you were spoiled! How many men?"

"Just one."

"Was it someone I know?"

"No," she replied. "And, Ebenezer, it wasn't how you think. I had no control—"

"All these years wasted! Fornication, dishonesty, betrayal—and God only knows how many other hidden sins. You...you've wasted my life!"

Annabelle swiped her tears away. "I would like to think that love is never wasted."

"How is love ever built upon a foundation of lies? Annabelle, you have struck with a dagger too deep. I cannot even recognize a notion of what reality once was. How could you? How...could... you?"

Annabelle stood and tried to go to him, but he pushed her away. "Ebenezer, I am so sorry. I have borne this secret—this curse—in silence."

"What curse?" Krow barked. "You made a choice to give your—"

"It was not my choice!" she shrieked.

"Enough!" Krow thundered. "Forget about my ill-advised marriage proposal. I was a fool. Forget about..." He reached into his pocket, withdrew the ring, and threw it with all his might toward the half-iced pond near the bridge. "Forget about the ring. Forget about us!"

"No, no! Ebenezer, please, listen. You don't understand!"

"I understand enough. Goodbye, Annabelle."

The senior Krow watched his younger self trudge off toward the bridge. When he got there, he let out a strangled cry and vomited into the water.

"You see?" the ghost asked.

"She had no right to keep that from me!" Krow barked, knocking the ghost's blade away with a fist.

"No," the spirit replied, "no, she didn't. And you had every right to cast her aside as if she was a lady of the night!"

"I'll thank you not to mock me."

"Your life mocks you," the ghost returned. "That is why I brought you here. Tell me, student of the Scriptures, does it ever trouble you that you know not what Annabelle meant when she said it wasn't her choice?"

Krow had no reply.

"One more journey," the spirit said, sheathing the blade once more. "And then, my time is finished."

"You torture me!" Krow screeched. "No more! I can bear no more!"

The spirit took hold of Krow's upper arm, and the wooded park slid out from under them. When Krow's wits returned to him, he stood just outside the gated driveway of a stately colonial home. It was dusk, and legacy snow remained in the nooks and crannies of the entire vista.

"Where are we?" Krow asked. "I cannot say that I have ever been here."

"Through the gate."

Krow hesitated but, seeing no alternative, trudged toward the tall wrought-iron bars—and right on through them! On the other side, a snowcapped hedgerow led around a bend, and Krow heard voices. A great many voices.

He raced ahead and found a gentleman, fresh from a shopping trip, it seemed, for he had prodigious, bulging black bags gripped tightly in each fist. Krow saw immediately why the man held the bags so secure, for a vortex of three boys and three girls spiraled around him, playfully pawing at the bags.

"Just what do you think is in these bags?" asked the man wryly.

"PRESENTS!" the children all shouted.

"Presents?" echoed the man. He turned his head and coughed twice. "Santa Claus needs no help from the likes of me. These bags are full of school supplies for the second semester."

"No, they're not!" an older boy shouted.

"You're cruel to us, Father," said the oldest girl.

Just then, the door to the home opened and shut, dispensing a womanly figure in great haste. With a curt, "Pardon me!" she gently brushed aside the children and wrapped her arms around the gentleman's neck.

"Careful, Belle," the man said, absorbing as many kisses as he could, "you might make me drop the pres—er, bags! Then, there would be chaos indeed."

"Then, Richard," she replied, "you'll just need to multitask."

When they separated at last, Krow recognized a much-matured Annabelle Prentice, but whatever else age may have done to her, it did not diminish her beauty. He blinked, again distracted by the six children, half of them in their early teens. "What a family she has now," Krow muttered. "Spirit, is this still the past?"

"Yes," it replied. "But not long past. Now, pay attention."

Krow felt like a schoolboy who'd just had his knuckles rapped by a zealous, ruler-wielding teacher. Still, he was obedient to the ghost's command.

"Back to your chores now, children," Annabelle said. "If we're finished by dinnertime, perhaps I will serve one of the pumpkin pies for dessert."

The kids scattered away and then funneled into the house, their Christmas joy clamor still audible even after the front door closed.

Annabelle took one of the bags from her husband, and the two slowly ambled, arm-in-arm, up the front walk.

"You know, I saw an old friend of yours in the city today," Richard said.

"Did you?" Annabelle replied, eyebrows raised. "Who was it?"

"Guess."

"Oh, husband, how can I? Wait, let me think. Downtown Manchester. Oh, I don't know—Ebenezer Krow."

"It was indeed Ebenezer Krow," he replied. "I was window shopping and happened by his legal offices. He was there, quite hard at work."

"On a Saturday?" Annabelle asked. "And on Christmas Eve? I suppose I should not be surprised."

Richard gave a dry chuckle, ending in a series of coughs. "Yes, well, he's rather renowned for his work ethic," he said, his voice a little raspy. "I'm told his partner, Marley Chastain, is in the hospital, quite close to death. I would have thought Krow would be there with him."

"That's only because *you* would be there for *your* friend," Annabelle said.

"Even so, Krow seemed content to work in his office, alone. He is quite alone in the world, isn't he?"

Annabelle paused on the front stoop. "Poor Ebenezer," she said. "Though I'm not certain I can genuinely feel proper sympathy for him."

Husband and wife went inside, and the clouds overhead darkened, leaving the scene enshrouded by shadow.

"Spirit!" Krow cried out, his voice cracking. "Remove me from here. I have seen enough—indeed, far too much. You need not haunt me any longer, for now, I shall be beleaguered by the thought that I might have been that husband to Annabelle, that that beautiful brood of children...might have been mine."

"The thought had occurred to me also," the ghost said, starting to turn his back to Krow. "And yet...you stood by your principles. You let the holy book guide your decisions. Can a man be blamed for that?"

"Take me home."

"You do not command me."

A kind of panicky fervor stole over Krow. He rushed forward, snatched the spirit's sword from the sheath, and brandished it toward his otherworldly guide.

"I command you now," Krow muttered. "Take me home, or feel both edges of this blade you are so keen to speak of."

"That's it," the ghost replied, bemused. "Let your ire rise and with it indignation. Consider the shadows of the things that have been. Dwell upon them. Dwell upon them, and use that blade as you see fit. Keep it. For it does not belong to me. I was merely the one who suggested how you might use it."

Brows beetling, eyes bulging, Krow rushed forward and drove the sword up, piercing the armor, piercing flesh and bone, and sliding into the ghost up to the hilt.

The ghost began to laugh, and its form began to dissolve. Krow no longer held the sword in his hands, but it was sheathed at his own side now. There came a clap of thunder. Startled awake, Krow became aware of his bedroom, particularly the floor, for that is where he lay. Exhausted and spent, he rose slowly, clambered into bed, and sank into a deep and dreamless sleep.

STAVE III
THE SECOND OF THE THREE SPIRITS

AWAKENING TO THE VIBRATIONS , of his own resound-
ing snores, Krow found himself in a most unusual bodily position. So tangled was it that he wondered how on earth he had
remained asleep. His upper torso was on its side, and he had
wrapped both arms around his shoulders in such a self-embrace
that both limbs had become quite numb. His lower torso, however, seemed to have its own mind and had taken a more leisurely
stance. One leg was half bent, making a kind of triangle pup tent
under the sheet. The other leg was exposed from any cover and
crossed over the knee of his first limb as if Krow was sitting at
ease, perhaps reading the news on the train.

   At once, he attempted to sit up, but his arms offered no
assistance. They were still mostly numb with a few areas be-
ginning to feel the pricks of pins and needles. Failing to gain
control of his arms, he managed to uncross his legs and swing
them over the side of the bed. He tried to use the movement's

momentum as a counterbalance to propel himself into a sitting position but, clever as the idea was, he failed. Limp arms flailing, he fell off the edge of the bed and landed hard upon the floor.

High-spirited aches flared to life in his already weakened hip, in both his knees, and especially on his right shoulder which had absorbed a most calamitous blow from the hardwood floor.

"Time is it?" Krow spluttered just as the bell of St. Marie began its sonorous toll. Once, twice, and no more.

"Two o'clock," Krow hissed, struggling to roll over. "The next ghost!" He craned his neck and stared around the dark room. No ethereal beings approaching that he could see. He wasn't sure what to expect as he flopped around on the floor like a fish in a bucket. I mean to tell you that Krow's imagination ran wild with him. Perhaps the second spirit would come in the form of a circus clown or an old doll with one eye missing. It could be anything from a warty troll to a baby with butterfly wings. Krow had set about to mentally prepare for anything, but he was not in any way ready for nothing. The bell had struck two, and no shape of any kind had appeared.

Krow began to tremble. His skin crawled, and the pins and needles spread across his arms. Four minutes passed. Five. At six minutes past, from beneath the door connecting to his library, a line of undulating crimson light blazed.

"Ebenezer Krow!" a hearty voice rang out.

Krow rocked back and forth. "Yes? I am here!" he called.

"Ebenezer Krow!" came the voice again, but louder and more insistent.

Krow managed to wriggle himself to the door. He used every working body part to shimmy into a seated position, his back to the door. "I'm here, I tell you! But I cannot get out!"

"Come in and know me better, man!" commanded the owner of that boisterous voice. "Come in, come in!"

"I...I'm trying!" Krow returned, but the blood still had not returned to his arms with enough volume. He swung each arm like a deadweight pendulum, trying to get his hand on the glass knob.

THE SECOND OF THE THREE SPIRITS

"Ebenezer Krow!" the voice cried out. "I am the second spirit that was foretold to visit you. We must not tarry!"

"I said, I'm trying!" Krow growled. On his ninth try, his right hand flopped onto the doorknob and took hold. Feeling like an idiot, he wrestled with his own arm, trying to wrench it in the right direction with his shoulder joint. Finally, he managed to turn the knob. He pulled the door open a few inches before it banged into his hip which, of course, was blocking the door's path.

"Do you need help?" called the ghost from the sitting room.

Krow sighed. "Yes, that...that would be nice."

Suddenly, Krow felt himself warmed as if by a glad fire in the hearth. Not only did the blood come rushing back into all of his limbs, but coursing energy too. He stood up and felt positively spritely. With great gusto, he heaved open the door.

Such a corona of blazing light came at him that he shielded his eyes. The radiance diminished—slowly—and Krow left his bedroom only to be dumbstruck by the apparition seated upon high.

It was Krow's library, yes, it was, but the seven bookcases were nowhere to be seen. In their stead, seated upon a throne of pine, fir, spruce, cedar, hemlock, and holly—a throne that Krow had neither owned nor seen before—was a being of Brobdingnagian proportions. Even seated, Krow could easily imagine this visitor to be ten, maybe twelve feet tall.

"You have never witnessed the like of me before!" bellowed the giant with a lusty laugh.

The spirit was garbed in a capacious robe that confounded Krow's attempts to name its color. One moment, it was a deep crimson. The next, it was dark green or blue or purple. The only color that maintained its hue was the white of the robe's fur border, which was open at the chest, revealing a very tanned and very muscular chest indeed. The ghost's hands, feet, and face were all so tan that it seemed the giant had been walking about beneath a bright sun for days on end. And like the sun, he held up a magnificent burning brand in his right hand. The happy light from that torch gilded the green garland upon his mane of fiery red hair. His brow, mustache, and full beard all matched that wily copper glow, and the expression upon the ghost's lively face was the very embodiment of joy. Though the ghost's amber eyes were warm and kindly, Krow found he could not endure them for long.

"No," Krow said finally, "I have never witnessed anyone like you before."

Still laughing, the ghost asked, "You have never fellow-shipped or supped or even walked about with the younger members of my family, my brothers and sisters?"

"No, never," Krow replied. "Or, at least, I cannot ever recall a being of your sort. Do you have a lot of siblings, Spirit?"

The ghost threw his head back and howled with laughter, saying, "Thousands of thousands!"

It was then that Krow noted the spirit's throne was surrounded by mountains of food and drink. There were crates of wine and kegs of beer. At least a dozen perfectly cooked golden turkeys fought for real estate with enormous hunks of steaming roasts. There were great vats of mashed potatoes, each with slabs of butter gliding down the contours like golden skiers on snowy slopes. Miles of sage sausages were strung together around the room like party favors. Pots of simmering string beans, asparagus, and other greens took up every end table and flat surface. Bubbling gravy boats, hot cross buns, decadent cakes, and fresh-from-the-oven pies gave the room so many glorious aromas that Krow's stomach growled audibly.

"I heard that!" the ghost roared. "Smell all you like, Krow, but do not touch."

"The many brothers and sisters you spoke of, is this feast, all this food and drink, for them?"

"Nay, Ebenezer," said the ghost. "These provisions are for all those you will see tonight and many more like them."

"Spirit," said Krow, ducking his head again, "the first ghost—though I did not like him nor wish to travel at his side—showed me things, things that are even now working upon me."

At Krow's words, the spirit began to guffaw so deeply that it shook the room like thunder.

Feeling himself the butt of some hidden jest, Krow asked, "Am I so funny as all that?"

The ghost reined in his uproarious laughter and said, "No, I am not laughing at you, nor the lessons you are learning. I am merely tickled fiercely by the Power at work tonight, and the means by which that Power has been expressed."

Krow said, "I do not follow."

"You will," the ghost replied. "Take a fistful of my robe!"

Krow followed orders, and throne, feast, and sitting room went away in a flurry of snowflakes.

Downtown Manchester rose up around Krow and his spectral guide: buildings tall and short, new and old, uniform and random—it was very familiar to Krow. But the Queen City on Christmas morning was a stunning landscape of newly fallen snow, Christmas decor, and people all bundled up, red-cheeked, and smiling.

The ghost gestured for Krow to follow and, together, they walked among the crowds. Many of the upscale shops, boutiques, and eateries were closed for Christmas, but those that stayed open were absolutely packed. "You see," Krow remarked, gesturing toward a local coffee shop that had a line of people around the block. "That's why I work on Christmas. People are still out and about."

The ghost rolled his eyes. "People are out meeting friends for a Christmas coffee. People are out for Christmas breakfast. People are out to get last minute Christmas gifts. I daresay people are not out for a Christmas lawsuit."

Krow wrung his hands and scowled, but hurried to keep up with the spirit whose strides covered thrice the ground Krow could manage even had he brought his cane, which he hadn't.

They passed a bus stop to the left where more than a dozen people waited, attempting to warm themselves but teeth still chattering as they spoke. Krow noticed as they passed these chilly souls, that the spirit lifted his torch above the bus stop and tilted it. Dancing pinwheels of gold poured out from the torch and descended upon the people waiting there, and immediately, they began to laugh. Just before they were out of earshot, Krow thought he heard them strike up a chorus of "We Wish You a Merry Christmas."

The ghost led Krow toward a famous coffee chain where the line, while not quite as lengthy as its competitor, was still fifteen people long outside of the door. The spirit lingered there a moment, just as a group of four ladies wearing heavy gowns, hijabs, and tentative expressions stepped into line. When they spoke, it sounded to Krow like some kind of Middle Eastern language. A few of those in line ahead of the women turned back briefly and, seeing them, quickly faced front. The ghost sighed deeply and passed over the entire line with his torch, unleashing a torrent of golden pinwheels. One of the women adjusted her hijab and smiled broadly. The whole line became much more animated: pats on the back, laughter—even a high five or two.

The spirit was off again, but Krow raced to take hold of the back of his robe. "Spirit!" Krow exclaimed, a decibel or two higher than he'd meant to. "Is there some special vigor or treatment that falls from your torch?"

"There is," the ghost replied, starting to walk again. "Given me to give to others freely and abundantly."

Krow bounded in front of the ghost to halt him once more. "But, Spirit, why there and why them? I mean, that coffee chain was in the news just last year for refusing to print 'Merry Christmas' on napkins and cups. And the Muslims? Spirit, they follow a different faith. Why waste—"

"You and I have very different ideas of waste, Ebenezer Krow. I deliver my salve to those who need it most. Do you think that Heaven smiles only upon Christians?"

"Well, I...that is, I mean to say that well, aren't they enemies of God?"

"What of it?" the ghost asked. "All mankind was an enemy to God."

Krow swallowed two counterarguments and managed a

weak, "If you say so."

"I do," the spirit said, but then he looked up as if he heard a happy melody no one else seemed to notice. "Ah, it is time. Listen."

Krow quieted his breathing and tried to perceive anything out of the ordinary, in which effort he failed, at first. And then, the bells of Manchester's churches began to toll.

With great glee, the ghost led Krow to a sidewalk with as good a view of downtown Manchester as anyone could get, aside from being atop a building. "Watch," said the spirit.

Krow watched. He saw normal traffic entering and exiting the circle. People continued to travel on foot this way and that. Perhaps, a few more cars took a particular road. Perhaps, a few more people ascended a certain sidewalk on a hill.

"Spirit, forgive me," Krow said, "but I'm not certain what I am seeing. Everything appears to me much the same as it did when we first arrived. What did you want me to look for?"

For the first time since they met, Krow found the ghost wearing an expression other than joyful warmth. The spirit's cheeks were reddened all right, and reddening more as each moment passed. His wiry copper brow was one big knot above the bridge of his nose, and his amber eyes simmered with new heat.

"There was a time, Ebenezer," the ghost said, words clipped with bitterness, "when the church bells would have rung, and people would have beaten a hasty pilgrimage to their sanctuaries for Christmas service. Public places such as this downtown area would become nearly vacant. It vexes me to see such a paltry return to the call for worship. What say you? Surely, with your penchant for following the letter of the law, seeing so many people with no intention of going to church must bother you?"

Krow immediately found the tops of his slippers extraordinarily interesting.

"Well, Krow?" The ghost's tone made it clear that he expected an answer and would brook nothing less.

"To be honest, Spirit," Krow replied timidly, "it would bother me exceedingly if it was a regular Sunday. But, I don't go in for service on holidays, especially Christmas. There's always some smarmy message about giving rather than receiving...or worse, a live manger scene with an inconsolable baby Jesus screaming at the top of his lungs."

The spirit crossed his arms and glared at Krow. "Your pedantic complaints aside, we will be attending your church today."

"What?" Krow blurted. "We can't. Not now. The bells have rung, and I cannot be seen coming late into St. Nicodemus. I'm an elder!"

"How many times must you be reminded? No one can see you, late or on time. Be that as it may, we will still arrive just in time. Calm your strident heart and take hold of my robe."

"Just in time for what?" Krow asked.

"My robe!"

Quick as lightning, Krow grasped the robe at the spirit's elbow. It was purple when he grabbed it but changed to dark green as Krow and the spirit materialized in the back of St. Nicodemus' sanctuary. The pews were three-quarters full with mostly white men, women, and some children, all dressed impeccably. An older gentleman stood at the lectern and, in a quaintly shaky voice, was giving an announcement about a potluck dinner being planned for the second Saturday in January.

"Where shall we sit?" inquired the ghost.

Krow whispered back, "I'd rather stand."

The announcements went on for another five minutes, and then a train of blue and white robed people came from an unseen door up front and dutifully filled in a lengthy set of risers to the far left of the pulpit. The worship leader, a man with a wedge of curly hair sticking out on either side of his head, raised his hands. All at once, the choir's collective voice rose in a pitch-perfect rendition of "Angels We Have Heard on High."

"Beautiful!" the spirit roared. "Aren't you going to sing, Krow?"

"Would it make any difference?" Krow replied. "They can't hear us."

"Quite right," the ghost replied, "but your singing is not *for them*."

Krow took the spirit's meaning and turned away. Noticing movement behind him, he looked on as one of the church's front doors opened, and a figure all in black entered. The person had unnatural plum-colored hair, a half-dozen piercings in one ear and one in the left nostril.

Krow frowned. This was not the sort of parishioner he was used to seeing at St. Nicodemus Church of the Holy Ghost. And the boots! Black knee-high boots with rows of spiky chrome studs! Krow muttered, "What is this, a heavy metal concert?"

The visitor moved quickly and furtively, sliding into a back row pew and slinging a large backpack onto the pew as well. An icy chill trickled down Krow's spine. Who brings such a hefty backpack to church? The chill bloomed into a full panicking blizzard. Visions of church shootings ricocheted around his consciousness.

Krow turned and tugged on the ghost's robe. "Spirit!"

"You're interrupting the music."

"But you're a spirit of benevolence, aren't you? You need to see this!"

Perturbed, the spirit turned. "What?"

"This person," Krow explained, gesturing to the visitor. "I...I think he might be armed and planning something wicked."

"Whatever gave you that idea?"

"Well, look at him! Do you see anyone else here dressed like him?"

"No," the spirit replied. "Indeed, I do not, and more's the pity. This person has come seeking."

While they were watching, a woman in a rigidly cut dress suit came around the row of pews.

"That's Gladys Perliman," Krow remarked, "the pastor's wife."

Mrs. Perliman knelt down discreetly at the visitor's side. "I'm sorry to disturb you," she said, "but I don't know you."

"I...I'm Sarah," the girl in black replied.

When she turned her head, Krow immediately recognized the person from the Bleak House Tavern, the androgynous one who'd worn all the colorful makeup. "It's a she," he muttered.

"Did you just call that lovely person an 'it,' Krow?"

Krow ignored the question and watched as Mrs. Perliman said, "Welcome to St. Nicodemus, but this is the regular service. The NA meeting is down in the basement."

Sarah went ghost white. "I'm not here for the NA meeting. I just wanted to see...well, I was hoping..." Her voice trailed off.

Mrs. Perliman's cheeks reddened. She said, "It's lovely that you're here, Sarah, but...well, the way you're dressed. I'm afraid you'll be a distraction."

"I was just leaving," Sarah said, narrowly missing Mrs. Perliman's hip as she swung her backpack round and raced out of the church.

Krow turned back to the spirit to find his eyes ablaze and his torch flaring. Krow swallowed deeply, fearing the ghost's kindling rage would be unleashed upon him. Just then, the final "In excelsis Deo" rose in a mighty crescendo, and the sanctuary fell silent.

To Krow's everlasting gratitude, the sudden ending of the singing distracted the spirit. They both watched as the choir rose as one and departed the same way they had entered.

"What?" the ghost objected. "Just one song? Is that the way of things here, Krow?"

"N-not always. Sometimes we have two...songs."

As an austere man in flowing robes ascended to the pulpit, the spirit said, "While their voices rang out, the Spirit of the Lord was here, Krow. The Almighty loves to inhabit the worship of His people, but such a brief welcome! Come, Krow, we have both seen enough. Take hold of my robe."

But Krow had turned away, staring at the church doors. He felt a pang of grief about the young woman who'd been turned away.

"Krow?" the ghost inquired. "Tell me your thoughts."

"I...I cannot," he replied quite honestly. "I am not certain how to put into words what I am feeling." Krow reached out and grabbed a fistful of the spirit's robe.

The sanctuary melted away, and all was darkness. Krow felt

movement and looked about for their next destination, but all he saw was that strange shimmering image of himself. This time, his blurry reflection was running after someone, but Krow could not see who it was.

When the darkness cleared, they were in a narrow alley between very old brick buildings. The glowering gray skies overhead threatened to add to the snow that had fallen the night before. "Where are we, Spirit?" Krow asked. "I do not recognize these dwellings."

"This is Varney Street."

"Varney Street? Varney...Varney, now why does that sound familiar?"

"Two reasons," said the spirit. "Some twelve of your years ago, your firm successfully litigated a suit which ended in the condemning of two buildings that had been used for low-income housing."

"Yes, that does ring a bell."

"The other reason is that your clerk lives here."

"Bob?" Krow objected. "In this part of town? Nonsense, I pay him better than that!"

"Come and let us see." The spirit carried his torch high, and as they passed by many doors, he wafted it about, spilling generous amounts of those golden pinwheels. Krow watched them dance and disappear, passing through those doors. He wondered what use the ghost's *seasoning* would be, how it might impact the unfortunates who lived in this downtrodden area.

"Ah," said the spirit. "Here we are. 22 Varney Street." Without another word, the ghost took hold of Krow by the wrist and led him through a small gate, up a slushy walk, and through the front door much as the pinwheels had done.

"Hurry, hurry!" Mrs. Craggett said to Eileen, the second of her three daughters as they both turned the corner and bounded down a curving stair. "We mustn't let our zeal for decoration be cause for an overcooked turkey."

Krow and the spirit followed down those same stairs and entered a kitchen positively bustling with cooking and cleaning and preparing—but all of it with eager merriment. Mrs. Craggett checked on the turkey, releasing a gush of steam.

"Mmmm," Mark the eldest son said, "smell the onion!"

"And rosemary!" Eileen replied. "Father's favorite!"

A vast pot jiggled on the stove's back burner, and the potatoes boiling within bobbed up to the surface, at times spilling a bit of water onto the stove with a hiss.

"Where is your father and Tom?" Mrs. Craggett asked, staring up at the clock.

"Chatting it up with Pastor Joe," Mark replied, dancing by with a dustpan and broom. "Doesn't he always?"

"True enough," Mrs. Craggett said. "But not so true that he would delay Christmas Dinner, would he?"

"If Daddy doesn't come," Avalynn, the youngest daughter asked, "can I have his potato?"

Mrs. Craggett whisked her daughter up into the air in a whirl of laughter and bouncing blonde pigtails. "You are a potato, aren't you?" Mrs. Craggett said. "A sweet potato!"

Just then, a door opened on the far side of the kitchen, and a tall, red-cheeked young woman entered, shutting the door briskly behind herself. In a blink, she'd shed her bulky coat, and said, "I could smell your string beans from a block away. Cooking them with a bit of bacon, aren't you?"

Mrs. Craggett put Avalynn down and rushed to embrace her oldest child. "Is there anything better?" she asked. "So glad the clinic didn't keep you, Kay but you won't be wearing scrubs to dinner, will you?"

"Oh, no," Kay replied. "I have an outfit picked out. It'll be quite festive."

As they separated, Mrs. Craggett eyed Kay suspiciously, and it was apparently well-deserved because Kay gave a rather impish smile before disappearing up the stairs.

"Daddy and Tom are coming!" Eileen announced, gazing through the window on the side door. "Let's prank them."

"What?" Mrs. Craggett blurted.

"Kay's upstairs changing," Eileen replied. "Let's pretend

she's not coming for dinner."

"You are a mischievous one," Mrs. Craggett replied. "But everyone must be in on it, shall we?"

The children assented and, a moment later, Bob came in, carrying Tom on his shoulder.

"Merry Christmas!" Bob and Tom crowed.

The rest of the family replied in kind.

"Do you smell this feast, Tom?" Bob asked.

"It's the bestest smell ever!" Tom exclaimed.

"Well, you both almost missed it," Mrs. Craggett said. "Bad enough that Kay can't make it."

Bob gently lowered Tom to the floor where he was quickly gathered up by his siblings who, being the conspirators that they were, proceeded to whisper in their little brother's ear.

His smile quickly shrinking, Bob asked, "Kay can't make it?"

Mrs. Craggett avoided her husband's eyes and took up a pair of potholders. "It's life in a medical clinic," she said, removing the potatoes from the stove. "You knew Kay was on call."

"I did?" Bob blinked. "But it's Christmas Day! How can our Kay not be coming on Christmas Day?"

"What do you mean I'm not coming?" And there was Kay, bouncing down the last few steps. She struck the most indignant hands-on-her-hips pose, but it was rendered hilarious by the grinning red-nosed reindeer on her most garish red and green sweater.

Both tricks exposed at once, the Craggett family positively shook the house with their laughter. Bob charged at Kay and lifted her up in a mighty hug.

"Get her, Big Bear!" Tom cheered.

Krow in an aside to the spirit said, "Did you see that sweater? How outlandish!"

"That seems to be the point," the ghost replied. "I've seen worse."

In the blink of an eye, the table was set, and the food delivered, creating steaming islands for all the young Craggetts to gawk.

Last came Mrs. Craggett with the golden brown turkey. She placed the platter before her husband to carve.

"Magnificent turkey, Mom," Kay said.

"It's ginormous!" Tom exclaimed.

"Yes, yes," Bob told his family, "we have been blessed both with the feast and your beautiful mother who prepared it. Let us pray and give thanks."

"You know that's really quite a small turkey," Krow whispered.

The ghost glared at Krow. "It's all Bob Craggett can afford."

"Spirit, here you speak out of turn," Krow said. "I pay Bob a fair clerk's wage."

"Krow, have you no eyes to see? The wage you call 'fair' might be fair to you, but to you only. And the medical insurance you provide—it's the worst of its kind. Have you any idea how much the experimental medicines for Tom's autoimmune disease treatments cost? Even with Kay's working at the clinic, the Craggett family is in financial ruin. Debtors calling by every means of communication."

"Gracious Lord," Bob began, "there is no adequate way to thank You for all You have done for us. On this precious day of remembrance, we worship You for who You are, and we offer our most heartfelt thanks for the blessings You've heaped upon us." And, at this, he paused and cast a furtive glance at Tom who, for his part, had his sweet eyes shut as hard as he could make them. "We are rich with every moment we share with each other and with You. May all that we do and say and press our minds upon bring a smile to Your holy face. In Jesus's name, amen."

"Amens" traveled the perimeter of the table, and Krow surprised himself by issuing his own audible, "Amen."

"What was that?" the spirit asked.

Krow looked again at the turkey, then at the potatoes, followed by the steaming string beans—any place but the spirit's eyes. He watched the Craggetts set about their meager feast as if it was a meal fit for the kings of old. Every mouthful was savored, and not the least crumb was wasted. At last when all was done and cleared away, Mrs. Craggett caught Bob under the mistletoe, and they shared a kiss that elicited *oohs* and *aahs* from all the children, young and old.

Then, she drew her husband away to a private corner only a pace away from where Krow and the spirit stood.

"How did Tom do...at church?" Mrs. Craggett asked.

His eyes already glistening, Bob said, "He was wondrous! He sang like an angel, listened to the sermon intently, and gave his little offering just as he promised he would. You know, he gets so thoughtful and asks remarkable questions. Why, as we filed out and gave our regards to Pastor Duke, Tom asked him if he thought that his body would be stronger in heaven than..." Bob's voice dropped off, and he and Mrs. Craggett held each other tightly and wept.

Krow gestured for the spirit to follow him away from Bob and his wife's most private moment. They stood in the stairwell, and Krow whispered, "Spirit, are you...are you permitted to tell me if little Tom will live?"

For just a moment, the ghost's torch seemed to falter, the flame diminishing to a soft glow. "I see an empty seat at this table," the ghost said, "a pair of crutches left ownerless but sacredly preserved in the corner by the fireplace. If these worldly shadows remain unchanged by the future, none other of my kind will find him here."

"No," Krow muttered, "no, no, good spirit, please say he will be spared."

"If these worldly shadows remain unchanged by the future, the child will die. What is that to you, Krow? If he is to die, perhaps he *should* die and remove the excessive drain on civil society once and for all."

Krow's misery was palpable, his own words choking him up and berating him like a circling multitude of demons.

"Gird yourself, man," the ghost hissed. "If man you are, renounce that vile hypocrisy until you have walked shoulder to shoulder with this 'excessive drain' to see where it is and who it is. Will you sit in judgment when the life of even a single soul sits in the balance? It may be that upon that scale, and in the sight of the Almighty, you, Krow—squanderer of gifts—weigh in as less fit to live than millions like little Tom."

Krow covered his face with his hands and trembled at the spirit's convicting words.

"Happy birthday to you," Mrs. Craggett began, carrying upon a tray a small cake with one lit candle.

"Happy birthday to you!" the rest of the family joined in.

"Birthday?" Krow mumbled. "Whose—"

"Happy birthday, dear Jesus! Happy birthday to you!"

"Oh," Krow muttered.

In addition to each tiny piece of cake, Mrs. Craggett brought round a motley series of mugs, and Bob came to fill each half-way with coffee.

"A very Merry Christmas to us all, my dear family," Bob proclaimed. "God bless us."

Tom, whose mouth was ringed with frosting, sang out, "God bless us and all the people of the world!"

Krow felt the spirit's heavy gaze upon him and turned.

"Come, Ebenezer," said the ghost. "For now, we must bid the Craggetts farewell."

"Oh, thank God," Krow replied. "I long for home with an inconsolable ache."

"Home?" the ghost echoed. "Did you honestly believe I was finished with you, Krow?" He held out his arm, and when Krow took hold of his sleeve, the ghost's laughter haunted his voyage through the darkness, all the way to the doorstep of a modest split-level home in Hooksett, New Hampshire.

"Do you know where we are now?" the spirit asked.

Krow scrutinized the home for clues. Two car garage, each with a snow-capped dormer above it, lots of double-height windows across the facade, and a happily smoking chimney on the left end. "No," Krow decided, "I don't think I've been to this home before. It...it looks like a nice neighborhood, suburb of Manchester, is it?"

"Yes," the ghost replied tersely, "and it is a nice neighborhood, made all the nicer because your nephew lives here."

"Fred?" Krow muttered. "His business must be doing quite well for him to be able to live here. Any suburb of Manchester is prime real estate."

With a little extra gusto, the spirit dragged Krow through the door and up a flight of stairs where a grand Christmas party was already in full swing. A crescendo of uproarious laughter drew Krow and the spirit to a long dining room table where no less than seventeen people sat.

"He said that?" asked a dapper but rotund fellow in a Christmas-spangled vest.

"On my honor, he did," Fred replied, wiping a tear from his eye. "When I wished him a 'Merry Christmas,' he replied with all sincerity, 'Bah! Hogwash!'"

The table erupted again. The silver garland that hung between a pair of chandeliers began to dance as if the laughter had sent small gales of wind into the air above the table.

"He said more beside," Fred went on, clearing his throat. "But I won't reveal all his words without him here to defend himself."

"Good for you, Fred," Krow said. "You've much better manners than the rest of these boors. And, Spirit, the only reason they laugh so hard is that they've no doubt consumed several drinks."

"That so?" the spirit inquired dubiously.

Ignoring the spirit as best he could, Krow turned back to the party.

A young woman in a deep-red dress sat across the vast table from Fred. She asked, "What did he say when you invited him to dinner?"

"The same thing he says every year, Mary," Fred replied, all the humor gone from his face. "It's very sad to me that he refuses. We are family. We ought to be together, if not regularly, at least for the holidays."

A dark-haired man in tweed jacket put his hand on Fred's and gave it a meaningful squeeze. "Well, we all know why he refuses to come, intolerant, tee-totaling, stick-in-the-mud that he is."

"No, Kevin, it's rather more deep-seated than that," Fred cautioned. "And my mother, God rest her precious soul, loved him dearly."

"You can't deny that our relationship has more than a little to do with his absence," Kevin argued.

"I do not deny it, husband," Fred replied. "But his aversions, I believe, are multifaceted. Like all of us, he bears his own scars."

Knowing murmurs traveled all around the table.

"You don't know what you're talking about, Fred," Krow hissed.

"Remember," the spirit chided, "he cannot hear you."

"Nor has he ever heard me," Krow groused. "After his mother died, he became the most ill-tempered, rebellious lad—"

"After his mother died," the spirit echoed. "Imagine that."

"I'll thank you not to sneer," Krow growled.

"The shame of it all," Fred went on, "is who does he harm by turning down all my invitations? Himself! And what does he miss? A grand time with lovely friends like you."

This time, a heartfelt, "Awwww," went round the table.

"I'll tell you what he misses," Kevin declared. "My most-righteous cooking!"

"Hear, hear!" the group shouted.

"Especially your decadent angel food fudge swirl," Mary said, reaching for a platter of desserts. "Speaking of which..."

During the ensuing laughter, Fred leaned to his husband. Their faces drew near—

"Dear God!" Krow croaked, turning away from the scene, his face contorting as if he'd just taken a sip of arsenic.

The spirit's torch vanished. He took Krow by both shoulders and bodily lifted him from the floor. He carried Krow around a corner and slammed him up against a linen closet door. "Dare you take the Lord's name in vain in my presence?" the ghost demanded. "Have you no shame?"

But though pained, Krow did not melt under this attack. "Have *I* no shame?" Krow argued. "Did you not just see my nephew committing blasphemy, indecency, and ungodliness? And you saw the rest of them—they practically ooze approval of it all. This world's gone mad, I tell you."

"The world has gone mad, Krow," the spirit agreed, "but

you're not helping!"

"How can you say that?" Krow returned. "The condoning of sin is much of the reason the world decays like it does. I study the scriptures, I am a witness of the truth, I pray, I go to church, I give."

"Hear me, Clanging Gong!" the spirit warned. "Student of the Word, do you remember when Jesus took care of the woman caught in adultery? You remember, He said, 'He who has no sin, cast the first stone.' You, my friend, have been casting stones most of your life. And do you even know why? You cast stones out of your own deep hurts. Parts of you, in the most ancient and abiding inner man, are broken, and you lash out at the injustice of what you've endured by condemning those around you. When you use the Almighty—yes, use Him and His word—to focus your castigating eye and your blistering words, you do so out of manifold emotions. Pain, hurt, fear, sorrow, spite, fury, rage, and insecurity—they all play you for a pawn. And you tell yourself that you are making a difference, that you are protecting those you reprove from future sin. Every single person in this room has secret hurt and yes, secret sin that is just as despicable, or more despicable, than the sins you can see. Your sins are just a subtly different shade of scarlet. Hurt does not heal hurt. Wounds do not heal wounds. Only love heals."

Krow blanched. He felt caught in a hurricane, pelted raw by the wind-driven rain. "But how can I love an unrepentant sinner?" Krow stammered. "Fred refuses to recognize homosexuality for what it is!"

"'For if while we were enemies of God,'" the spirit quoted, "'we were reconciled to God through the death of His Son...'"

"Are you saying Fred is not sinning?"

"Nothing of the kind, Krow," the spirit thundered. "Are you saying you are not sinning?"

"You are rationalizing!"

"Hard-hearted man, you are not listening! Do not mistake love for approval of everything a loved one does and thinks!"

"Isn't it?" Krow retorted, his words catching in his throat.

"Oh, Ebenezer, don't you understand? It is only by genuinely investing in the lives of others that you earn the right to speak truth to them? Instead, you use truth as a club, hoping to beat and shame others into the kingdom. That isn't how the Master does it. He loves generously and unconditionally. Are you better than the Master? You must love *first*."

"And how would you suggest I love my misguided nephew?"

The spirit removed his right hand from Krow's shoulder, and the fiery torch reappeared in it. "'Love is patient, love is kind and is not jealous; love does not brag and is not arrogant...'"

Fred's home vanished in a vortex of shadow. Krow pondered many things as the blind motion took him once more. The spirit's words rang over and over in his mind. *Could the ghost be right?* he wondered. *Wait! What was it that Chastain told me? Three messengers, but one of them is something devilish, something that seeks to do me harm.* The Spirit of Christmas Past had been grim and forceful, to be sure, but had taught Krow many things, reminded him of things he ought not to have forgotten. The ghost guiding him now, the Spirit of Christmas Present, seemed a merrier sort, but there was something hard as flint beneath his jovial nature. But was it something sinister? He did seem to be advocating sin. Krow wasn't sure. He resolved to discover the villain once the third spirit appeared. Surely, by comparison, it would be a simple matter of evidence and conclusion.

Krow felt a sudden tug but not from the spirit. Whatever it was pulled Krow free of the spirit's grasp and sent him cartwheeling sideways—or at least, what felt like sideways without any visible point for reference. "Help!" he cried as he careened past a glimmer of light.

Then, he saw once more the blurred reflection of himself, like some kind of ethereal replay of everything he'd experienced with the ghosts of the past and present. Scene after scene, Krow saw himself and cringed. Some of the visions had changed, displaying Krow in the worst light possible. One moment, he saw himself dressed in flowing robes, screaming obscenities at Jesus in the den of sinners. A blink later, he saw the old rectory door where his younger self emerged from Levesque's study carrying a bloody hatchet.

"Nooo!" Krow screamed as he watched himself deliver a devastating open-handed slap to Annabelle's tear-streaked face.

"That's enough!" came a voice like thunder, and Krow felt an iron grip take hold of his left arm. For a moment, he thought he might be pulled apart by the two mighty factions, but at last, the presence on the right side let go.

Krow found himself standing next to the Spirit of Christmas Present in a shadowy alleyway. Trembling and barely able to speak, he pleaded with the ghost, "Please, tell me what that was that I saw."

The spirit held his torch aloft above Krow's head and let fall his golden essence. "Alas, Ebenezer," the ghost said, "as much as I know you and your ways, I almost feel sorry for you. Breathe; breathe deeply, and know that I will keep a better hold of you from now until the end of our time together. I deeply regret to tell you that I am not permitted to speak of what you just experienced or what it might mean. Know this, Krow: just as the hands of the clock wind ever forward, you also are moving forward. And the meaning of what you've seen will be revealed in due time."

"Your words, they do not bring comfort," Krow said, "but I feel the work of your torch's light upon me. It strengthens me. Please, Spirit, lead me where you will. I will listen. I will learn. I...I will try."

"We travel now along the streets of Manchester, particularly in the areas between streets named for trees: Spruce, Cedar, and Beech."

Krow hurried to keep up, and they came to a clinic where at least a dozen children sat on the concrete steps outside. As he passed them, he saw their breath, heard their wheezing and hacking coughs. And he saw that they were dressed in rags and clinging to each other for warmth.

"What is this place?" Krow asked. "I have never seen the like."

"No, you haven't," the ghost replied. "This is a medical clinic, staffed by volunteers mostly. A few respiratory therapists are on duty tonight."

"But it's Christmas," Krow said, "and all these; well they're just kids. They shouldn't be exposed like this."

"'Are there no shelters?'" the ghost asked. "'Are there no group homes?' See for yourself, Ebenezer; these are the poor of Manchester. There are nearly three thousand children living well below the poverty threshold as your worldly politicians are fond of calling it. They suffer from malnutrition, uncontrolled asthma, and lead poisoning."

"Lead poisoning?" Krow barked. "I thought that ended at the turn of the century."

"Nay, Krow, and there is worse still. Pray, be silent and watch."

They turned down a trash-strewn street, past half a dozen decrepit, hollow-eyed buildings. In every corner, in every recess, in every place where a human form could fit, people huddled. Some were wrapped in layers of threadbare clothing, but most used cardboard or half-full trash bags for warmth and shelter. Some of them lay unconscious, the skin of their faces pressed onto the cold brick walk.

A shrill scream made Krow jump. He looked about but saw no source, no movement. Angry shouts, like gunshots, issued forth from dark side streets. Krow felt the urge to run, but the spirit kept him at pace.

At last, they turned a corner and stood near a street lamp on the verge of burning out. The spirit moved under the flickering white light and said, "The people you've seen, Ebenezer Krow, are your brothers and sisters. They are the 'least of these' spoken of by the Lord. I wonder, have you clothed them? Have you fed them? Have you even given them a cup of cold water to drink?"

Krow felt nauseous. He trembled and stared downward. Then he gasped and backed a few paces away. "Spirit," he cried. "I see something hidden... hidden at your feet beneath your garments. Is there a limb of some kind, a claw?"

"Look here," the spirit commanded. And from the folds of his robes, he revealed two wizened creatures. They were a boy and a girl, but so shriveled and scaly that all humanity was gone from their wretched countenances. Their eyes bulged from caved-in sockets, and they sniffed about like sewer rats. Then, slowly, the boy lifted one limb—an arm—and its nearly skeletal hand unfolded until one finger pointed at the girl. And they both began to hiss and spit.

Krow began to back away, but he managed to croak out a question: "Are these yours?"

"They are the offspring of Man," said the spirit, staring down upon them in the strobing light. "They leech upon me, draining away the very marrow of my bones. The boy is Judgement. This girl is Fear. Beware them both and beware all like them, for there are many clinging to you right now."

Krow let out a sort of squeal and searched himself but saw nothing.

"Most of all, take caution for this boy, for upon his brow I see the writing of damnation!"

In the distance, a church bell rang out the toll of the hour. One chime. Then two. And finally...three. Krow looked about the street for the ghost, but he was gone.

As the reverberating toll of three ceased, Krow felt a presence behind him. He spun and saw a sea of low mist cresting the hill and rolling down toward him. There appeared a hooded apparition, hovering at the top of the hill. It was draped in shrouds that writhed all about its form. And from beneath its hood, red eyes shone forth.

"No!" Krow cried out. "This is no devilish spirt. This is the devil himself come to claim me for his own!"

STAVE IV

THE LAST OF THE THREE SPIRITS

KROW TURNED TO RUN but managed only a few steps before being stricken in place. Vaporous, muddy-gray skeletal hands lifted him up and restrained him by the shoulders, arms, and legs.

Their grasp was chilling and irresistible, reminding Krow of Chastain's writhing cold fire. In that moment, he lost all manner of dignity. Shrieking, crying, and flailing, he tried to escape, but more of the cadaverous hands appeared and took hold of him. In addition to dignity, Krow nearly lost control of his bodily functions when one of the bony tendrils clamped upon his mouth. It numbed Krow's lips and felt both like cold iron and damp soil.

"Cease your struggling," came a voice from behind, if a voice it could be called, thin and dry, sibilant and otherworldly—more like to a chorus of spectral voices, each one oscillating as if struggling for supremacy. "Cease your struggling, and they will... depart from you."

Krow froze in place and, one by one, the hands dissipated.

The last to release was the one that had covered his lips. Krow spluttered and spat, trying in vain to relieve that deathly sensation from the flesh of his face. The rolling fog spilled around and between his feet, continuing to flow downhill as if on a private errand known only to itself.

Krow felt a presence behind him. "Are you the third spirit?" he asked, his voice quavering. "The Spirit of Christmas Yet to Come?"

"I...am."

In spite of the fear gnawing at him like rats upon bone, Krow turned around to face—but it was gone. Krow gasped. The sea of fog still flowed, but the specter was no longer there. And yet, it was. Krow could feel it. "Spirit, you are going to show me shades of things that have not happened but will come to pass? Is this your business with me?"

Krow turned back downhill. Red eyes flared just inches from his own, and the hooded figure replied, "Yes... it is."

To say Krow jumped backward would be understatement akin to calling a dead man, merely sleeping. So startled and terrified was he that he vaulted some six feet away from the spirit. Krow fell to his knees and held up his entwined hands. "Spirit," he cried, "I have felt no comfort in the company of any of the specters who've visited me tonight, but I fear you the most. If I am to venture out with you, I need your assurance that what you will show me will be for my own good and not for my destruction."

The ghost did not reply but straightened to its full height, and that was tall indeed. It was not broad or full like the gigantic second spirit but was rather a stretched form, bony, angular, and emaciated. The ever-moving black hooded cloak rippled over its body, revealing shapes that Krow tried very hard not to recognize.

"Spirit, please, I plead with you for assurance. I...I don't think I can will myself to move...without it."

The spirit raised an arm out to its side, and a gnarled hand emerged from its tattered sleeve. No sooner did its segmented fingers extend than a long black stave appeared in its grasp. At the top of the shaft, a long, sickle-shaped blade curled out like razor-sharp talon.

With its other hand, the spirit pointed at Krow and then curled its fingers in a beckoning motion. "Come," it said.

"But, spirit—dreadful revenant—I am paralyzed by fear!"

"Would you rather be carried?" the spirit rasped and, in an instant, a veritable squadron of those vaporous skeletal hands appeared in front of Krow.

Krow found his vigor then, I can tell you. He leaped up from his knees. "No, no!" he squawked. "I think...I think I can manage. Please, send them away."

Something like a laugh rattled out of that darkened hood, and its eyes smoldered like embers from a fire nearly spent. To Krow's potent relief, the skeletal hands vanished.

The apparition turned and gestured with its scythe for Krow to follow, and he obeyed. With every step, the fog thickened and rose up. Just as it enveloped him, the mist cleared away, revealing the gray facade of a monument-like building.

"Spirit, you've brought me to the district courthouse."

The ghost nodded.

"I'm glad for once to be at a place so familiar," Krow said. "If you had any idea how much time I've spent here."

"Inside," the spirit hissed.

"I'm going. I'm going," Krow said, and he hurried toward the revolving door. He glanced back over his shoulder to find the spirit not walking but flowing rapidly behind him. Krow sped up his pace and entered the building. The cavernous courthouse lobby was abuzz like a stirred hornets' nest. The foot traffic moved along briskly, except for a line at the security post.

Armed police officers frisked people, required them to empty pockets, and place laptops and bags on the x-ray rollers. The officers sent each person, one at a time, through the upright metal detector. Out of habit, Krow got in line.

"Foolish man," the spirit said. "You are not corporeal. Go through."

Krow did as he was told, and walked right past the police offi-cers and their equipment. There were no shouts, no alarms. Krow was rather relieved, thinking for a moment that the spirit would have a difficult time getting by security with that scythe.

The two ethereal visitors passed silently through the any-thing-but-silent hall, and Krow found himself catching snippets of conversation.

"The police haven't released the details," one rather corpu-lent fellow said to another.

"But he is dead?" the other replied. "You're certain of that much?"

A few paces later a severe woman in black was saying, "I don't suppose there was foul play. 'Old is old,' as they say."

"But what a hoot if it was," a petite woman with owlish eyes replied. "There'd be no end of suspects."

Krow glowered at the women, a glare he'd perfected on ju-ries he'd wanted to intimidate, but it had no impact at all. Krow saw that the spirit had taken quite a lead and hurried to catch up. The spirit halted at a small circle of suited men and women. Krow knew a few of them by name, and yet, there were several Krow had not only never seen but felt most assuredly that they could not be nearly old enough to serve the district court in any capacity whatsoever.

"At four, I believe," said David Swavely, a highly respected prosecutor.

"Where?" asked one of the young men.

"Saint something," David replied.

"Starts with an N, if I'm not mistaken," said a paralegal named Vivian Scarborough. "Saint Nick's, Saint Nixon..."

"Saint Nixon!" David blurted out in a hearty laugh. "Now, that would be a church I could attend!"

"Saint Nicodemus!" an older legal recruiter Krow knew as Deborah B. Felchings said. "It's over on Wellington."

"Ha!" Krow said aside to the spirit. "She used to be in the church choir. We used to call her 'Little Debbie' because no one could believe such a loud voice could come from such a petite old woman."

"Are you going?" David asked.

"Most likely," Little Debbie replied. "It'll be nice to see the old place, quite stately."

"We don't have to go, do we?" a young woman asked. "I have plans."

"No, no," David said, "this is not so important an event as all that, but he was a fixture here for nearly forty years. I'll be going. I hear they're serving a buffet lunch."

"More importantly," Vivian said, adjusting her collar that seemed to be squeezing her slender neck, "what's going to happen to the firm?"

A pall of silence fell over them all for a few moments, each of them casting furtive looks to the others.

"Who can say?" David replied. "I'm told he bought out his partner's stake, but he had no living relatives."

"It'll probably go on, business as usual," Little Debbie said. "That's the way he'd want it, you know."

"But they don't really have a real draw anymore," Vivian said. "No one quite as effective."

"Ruthless, you mean," David said mirthlessly.

"I think I might know a few who could fit that bill," Little Debbie replied.

"It'll all come out in the wash," David said. "I'm off now. Good bye."

The circle scattered, and Krow looked up to the spirit. Forgetting his terror for a moment of indignation, he said, "Spirit, why did you bring me here? And why to hear such conversations as this? The previous spirits recognized the brevity of their time."

"You speak ironies," the spirit grated. "Ironies made all the more ironic by your lack of comprehension."

"But I don't see what this has to do with me—"

"Take hold of my scythe."

Eyeing that fearsome blade, Krow sighed and obediently took hold of the stave. The district court burned, but not to the ground. Blue flames started at the floor and feverishly climbed, consuming everything, ceiling and all.

In its place, there came a claustrophobic alley, and Krow thought he knew it. But distracted by three shadowy forms, he didn't voice his thoughts. They were not spirits but were covered head-to-foot in black. They moved quickly and purposefully, stopping at the lock of a wrought iron fence that guarded an old Victorian building. Tools came out, glinted briefly, and the gate flew open.

"What is the meaning of this?" Krow demanded.

The spirit stood impassively by and said nothing.

At the back door of the home, the trio took pause. It was so dark that Krow could scarcely tell the difference between the invaders and the night. But here and there, a star point of green or red light blinked. There came a sudden crash. Instantly, floodlights came on, and a spectacular klaxon alarm rang out.

In full view now, the three burglars raced into the house. The alarm continued to wail, but there was no sign of a response. No distant sirens. Nothing.

"What's going on here?" Krow bellowed. "Someone should do something!"

The spirit lifted his scythe and began to whirl the blade high in the air. Krow watched as a tendril of night descended in a tight funnel, rotating with the motion of the sickle blade.

"No, wait!" Krow cried out. "We can't let them get away with this!"

The vortex widened, and there came a deep rumbling. Krow backed away a few paces. The back door of the house crashed open, and the three burglars burst out, each carrying a large black bag. They raced through the gate, but making the turn into the alley, the last of their crew dropped something.

Krow watched the dark figure reach down. He picked up some sort of cane or walking stick. Krow saw a glimmer of silver, but the criminal tucked the object away and raced out of the floodlight's coverage.

Krow went to follow the thieves, but the vortex of night

overcame him. When the shroud cleared, Krow saw rectangular room dimly lit by pale utility lights on either end. It was a sterile chamber filled on either long wall with evenly spaced metal gurneys, wide multi-faucet sinks, and tilting disc-light fixtures hanging down on jointed arms.

The spirit's arm thrust forward, startling Krow yet again, and pointing to the far side of the room.

"Spirit," Krow huffed, trying to catch his breath. "Where is this place? It looks like a hospital. Are we visiting Universal Medical? I don't like it here. It's cold and reeks of antiseptic chemicals."

The spirit continued to point. "5-E..." it rasped.

Krow stumbled forward, glanced back, and noticed it had been several of those ethereal hands that had given him such a thrust. He knew better than to delay, so he traversed the chamber, keeping his eyes straight ahead and his mind busy with anything but his present circumstances. When he reached the opposite end, a monolithic silver refrigeration unit rose up before him. It was sterile silver, six square doors across, four down. On the far left was a digital master control panel, and a series of intake fans whirred quietly on top.

Krow noted and recognized the structure. Combined with the gurneys and sinks, he realized where the spirit had brought him. It was a morgue. "Spirit," Krow said, shaking his head slowly, "I do not wish to be in this place. I take your meaning. The end is near for all of us, and my own likely closer. I will not forget the lesson, but bear me from this place."

The spirit had made no sound, but that hideous rolling fog now ran along the floor of the chamber. The spirit stood in a writhing pool of it, not six feet from Krow. "5-E..." it said.

Krow trembled visibly. He'd noted the number-letter designation on each of the silver doors. Involuntarily, his eyes found 5-E. Krow's stomach churned, and some bizarre corner of his disturbed mind was reminded of the pantry freezer in the basement of his home. The thought brought on new waves of nausea, and he stepped aside.

"No, Spirit," Krow muttered. "I cannot. If this door must

open, then you must open it."

Beneath that dark hood, the red eyes flared like struck match heads. The spirit regarded Krow for a very long time, and the old lawyer felt his old heart beat an irregular cadence. The spirit raised his scythe and then smacked the butt of it to the floor.

The door to 5-E opened. Fluorescent blue-tinted lights blinked stubbornly to life. A form lay covered within, one foot partially escaping the heavy sheet. The spirit pointed, and a trio of spectral hands appeared. The hands took hold and effortlessly drew out the tray. The lights within continued to flicker as the body slowly emerged from its climate-controlled place of rest. Krow saw a tag dangling from the corpse's exposed toe and lest he read anything written upon it, he took a long step backward.

The skeletal hands vanished, and the spirit commanded, "Lift... the sheet."

Krow recoiled as if he'd been struck. "L-lift the sheet? No, no, there's no need. What right have I to disturb the dead?"

"You took the ring from Chastain's finger," the spirit hissed. "Lift...the...sheet."

Krow remembered Marley Chastain on the slab. He remembered taking the ring back. He remembered Chastain's bloodshot, cataract-occluded eyes and a perilous thought took hold of him. *Wretched, cold finger of death,* he thought, *none escape your touch. It is given once for man to die...*

"...And then to face judgment," the ghost finished aloud.

In that moment, Krow felt utterly exposed, for he could no longer hide, not even in his own thoughts. The spirit saw through and through. Krow's body trembled. His arms trembled. His lips trembled, and he could barely stutter out the words, "Merciful Heaven, I cannot lift this veil! I have not the strength. I would if I could manage it, but something tells me that to perform this deed would be my undoing. I cannot do it. I cannot—"

The spirit's shriek pierced every other sound, climbing in pitch and intensity until becoming a scathing, scraping wail. The body of 5-E careened back into its enclosure, and the door slammed behind it. All at once, other doors began to open. Amidst blinking lights, other corpses began to emerge but each for only a moment. Two at a time, then five at a time, then one, then three. There was no pattern. The spirit's banshee scream continued to rise. Krow cowered away from the doors, but something told him to keep watching.

Thunder clapped, and but for 5-E, every single door flung itself open. The trays all slid out in unison, and in unison, the corpses sat up, dropping their sheets from their emaciated faces. They turned as one and pointed to Krow.

"Enough!" Krow cried out. "Spirit, there is too much death, too much dire threat—it is all too heavy a burden to bear. Please, take me somewhere—anywhere—where there might be some tenderness, some compassion, some brave hope!"

The ghost waved its scythe once, and the morgue melted away, leaving behind an older, darker, more disheveled 22 Varney Street.

Krow found the spirit standing by Bob Craggett's door. "There must be some mistake," he said. "I have already visited this home tonight. I have not forgotten it, nor will I ever."

The spirit made little sound but vanished through the front door. Krow hurried to catch up, jogging the icy walk carefully, and then passing through the door to the landing between stairways. And though it looked the way it had on his previous visit, Krow felt something had changed. It was as if the air itself had gotten heavier or the gravity had increased as it might on a different planet. He did not immediately see the spirit, so he shuffled down the stairs. As he hit the bottom step, he saw the last few inches of that sickle blade pass beyond the kitchen and into the living room.

In that room, Krow found the ghost, somehow shrunken, standing in the corner of the room, nearly blending into the bookcase and its motley collection of old tomes. Mrs. Craggett was also in the room, sitting on the couch with her knees up to her chin and sipping at a steaming mug. Most of the children were there too, seated in somber pairs on bench seats.

Krow could not fathom the change that had come over the whole family. They were so very quiet and still. Even the meager fire whispered in its grated keep.

"Read it again, Mark, would you?" Mrs. Craggett asked.

The eldest son pursed his lips and nodded. He lifted an open Bible from a nearby end table and traced a finger down a page of script. "'The righteous cry out, and the Lord hears them; he delivers them from…all their troubles.'" Mark stopped a moment, cleared his throat, and soldiered on. "'The Lord is close to the brokenhearted and saves those who are crushed in spirit.'"

Mrs. Craggett put down her mug and covered her face with her hands.

"Do you want me to read it again, Mom?" Mark asked.

"No, no," Mrs. Craggett replied, her voice cracking. She slowly lowered her hands, revealing very red eyes. "I think I have it memorized by now."

"Oh, Mom," Eileen called out, "you're wearing red eyeliner again."

"Yes, I seem to be wearing it often these days," Mrs. Craggett replied. "Come here, my little beauty."

Eileen's slippers made no sound on the floor. She clambered up onto the couch and cuddled in close to her mother. "That's better," Mrs. Craggett said, dabbing her eyes with the hem of one sleeve. "Perhaps, now I can be done with the red eyeliner. I wouldn't dare show red eyes to your father. It must be about his time."

"Past it, I think," said Mark, closing the Bible. "But I think he's been so lost in thought of late that he's missed the bus again. He told me so just the other evening."

The room went quiet once more. Mrs. Craggett eventually looked up and said, "Some things change and yet stay the same. Your father used to come late because he and Tom were off on some adventure or other. I've known your father to carry Tom all 'round downtown Manchester just to let him pick up a bag of penny candies."

"I remember," Mark said.

"So do I," said Kay.

"And I," said Eileen.

"Daddy used to twirl Tom about as they walked," Avalynn said. "He was lighter than me."

"Shh!" Kay cautioned. "Father's here at the door."

Bob came in as bundled as he could be. Slowly, he made himself visible, removing his trapper hat, then unraveling a thick scarf, and finally removing a coat so heavy that it nearly toppled one of the kitchen chairs.

"Oh, Bob," Mrs. Craggett said softly, "come in, come in. I have a plate in the oven for you."

Bob hugged his wife as a drowning man might clutch a life vest. "Thank you, my darling," he said. "But not...not just yet. I don't think I can eat yet."

"Well, come and sit with us then," she said. "We're all here by the fire."

Bob moved unsteadily—nearly staggered—to the high-back cracked leather chair nearest the hearth. Mrs. Craggett whisked little Avalynn up from her place on the couch and settled her onto Bob's lap. The bright spark of sunshine that she was, Avalynn smiled up at her father, took his hands, and fastened them around herself like a seatbelt.

"Ah, my dears," Bob said. "To be with you all at Christmas... I can think of no greater gift from our Lord. I told Pastor Joe that."

"You went by the church?" Mrs. Craggett asked. "To talk to Joe?"

Bob stared into the fire. "Bless his heart," he said. "He agreed to meet me to talk things through... and to cry. I told him he didn't have to stay, that I could visit...visit Tom on my own, but he wouldn't hear of it. Do you know what he did? He embraced me and said such a prayer for me and for all of us that I shall never forget. Tom always loved Pastor Joe's prayers."

At this, Bob began to crumble in on himself. "My Tom, my Little Bear...my sweet son!" His breakdown would have been a shattering thing to see were it not mitigated by all of the Craggetts at once. They surrounded Bob and hugged him mightily.

They wept, and they whispered, and they clutched each other.

"Spirit," Krow whispered, "something tears at my heart and steals the strength from my voice. I asked you to take me to a place where I might see tenderness and compassion. And though I rue the occasion, I have seen it and more. Poor little Tom. Poor Bob."

The hooded spirit's eyes dimmed to barely smoldering slits, but he made no move to leave the home.

The Craggetts peeled away, one by one, and Bob, though red-eyed and careworn, managed an honest smile. "Do you know who else I saw today?" Bob asked. "On the bus?"

Mrs. Craggett cleared her throat and said, "I'm sure I can't imagine."

"I saw Kevin Marwright," Bob said, "or rather he saw me. And though we've only met a few times, he was kind enough to inquire after us."

Mrs. Craggett blinked a few times. "I think I remember him now," she said. "He was Fred Bithywell's hus—"

"Yes," Bob replied quickly. "He and Mr. Krow's nephew had a relationship. In any case, he said that he noticed I looked a little down and wondered what could have me in such a state on Christmas. I told him. I told him probably far more than he wanted to know, but he was the kindest, most understanding gentleman I think I have ever met, for he said, 'I am most heartily sorry for your loss, Mr. Craggett. Heartily sorry for you, your good wife, and your children.' He wasn't finished either. He actually said, 'If I can offer you and your family any help, anything at all, please call on me.' And then, he handed me his business card."

"What a kind soul," Mrs. Craggett observed.

"He wasn't finished yet," Bob said. "Before I could object, he asked for our address and said he would bring us his world-famous lasagna for a dinner sometime this week."

"I love lasagna!" Mark blurted.

"Don't we all?" asked Bob.

"Oh, I hope it's a night I'm not working," Kay said.

"We'll make sure that it isn't," Mrs. Craggett assured her. "What a kind person."

Each of the Craggetts nodded, and they sat for a few moments in companionable silence.

"Speaking of work," Bob said at last. "Mark, you'll be starting at the grocery after break, won't you?"

Mark nodded vigorously. "Three evenings in a row," he said. "They're low on cashiers now. Worst time around the holidays. I'll probably have to work quite a bit."

"Ah, Mark," Bob said, "you are becoming quite the young man, aren't you? And Eileen, it won't be long before you will be thinking about work."

"Don't rush them out the door, Bob," said Mrs. Craggett.

"Oh, I'm not. I'm not," he said, making a sweeping gesture with his arms. "It's just that...well, time continues to march on, and sooner or later, there will be times when we must part with one another. Whenever that must be, I know in my heart that none of us will forget our Tom, even though he is parted from us for now."

"We won't forget," Mark said, followed by the same from each of the other Craggetts.

"My heart also tells me," Bob went on, "that when we remember Tom, you'll think of how he earned his nickname, Little Bear. We'll remember how brave he was against a wicked enemy. Then we ourselves will not find it easy to quarrel with one another, for we will remember Tom and remember that none of us are the enemy."

"We'll remember, Daddy," little Avalynn said, and all followed her lead.

Bob did nothing to fight his tears. "You have all made me...a happy man, this Christmas. Do you hear? A very happy man."

Mrs. Craggett started a parade of kisses upon her husband. When it was Mark's turn, he held out a hand for his father to shake. Bob took that hand, but yanked his son in close and gave him several whiskery kisses on the cheek. They all laughed.

"Spirit," said Krow, "I see now why we lingered, for you

have now shown me the last thing that I asked for: brave hope. I have seen it, and I know it. But something tells me there is still unfinished business ahead. I don't know how I know, but I know. And I am afraid, but there is something else at work in me. Lead on, Spirit."

The ghost tapped the scythe shaft to the floor once. The Craggetts and all of Varney Street vanished in a blur. A cobbled stone lane appeared ahead, curling around a massive, ever-rising hill. Krow couldn't tell what it was, for the night was too dark. There was no moon above and very few stars. Krow shivered, for it was deathly cold. Remnant snow clung to the trees on that hill, and icicles formed in an orderly row along...along a fence. Yes, it was a fence. Krow could see it now, due to the ice. And no wonder he hadn't seen the fence at first, because it was black wrought iron. It ran all along the lane but seemed to disappear around the bend.

"Spirit," Krow asked, "where are we?"

The spirit did not reply, but its eyes blazed once more. It reached out its arm and pointed ahead. Krow hesitated for a moment only, knowing that if he didn't move, surely the unearthly skeletal hands would appear to *assist* him. It was a tentative, stumbling walk for Krow as he looked this way and that through the fence, and then back to the spirit following close behind.

Little by little, Krow's eyes began to adjust to the darkness and, as he stared through the fence, shapes a shade less dark than the black mass of the hill began to emerge. He thought he saw human forms and pillars, oblong altars, and pale houses.

"Please, Spirit," Krow implored, "of all my destinations this night, I have never felt a menace like this. It freezes the marrow of my bones and warns me of violence."

Still, the ghost did not answer. It moved along without walking, and always, that inexorable finger pointed forward.

As they cleared the bend, Krow saw a vast stone arch rising up from the fence line. Closer still, Krow read the name written in iron tracery upon that arch: Sojourners Memorial Cemetery.

If Krow had any iron in his gut or steel in his will, he lost both then. He began to collapse, but a sortie of the ghost's dismembered hands picked him up and ushered him through the cemetery's opening gate. Krow swooned as they traveled a winding gray path through the graveyard, passing crosses, headstones, monuments, and mausoleums. Black, leafless trees crowded in from either side and shrouded the view overhead in jagged netting.

Krow began to collect his mind once more, and he attempted to gain mastery over his limbs as well. But the grip of those hands was irresistible. A few inches above the ground, they bore him, even while he struggled.

"Confound you!" he shouted. "Let go of me!" To his surprise, they did, vanishing in an instant. Krow stumbled to right himself and then strode on, brushing himself off as if soiled.

"Turn...here..." the ghost's voice snaked out of the darkness. Krow looked back over his shoulder to see the spirit pointing out into the sea of woods and headstones.

"But the path doesn't turn here," Krow said. "There is only brier and deadfall."

"Turn."

Krow obeyed and crunched upon dead leaves, branches, snow, and even a few pine cones. The way led up a slight incline and wove around many graves. Krow steered very clear of these and, as they passed farther from the path, he felt the frostbitten blade of terror take hold of him once more.

"Spirit," he called out, his voice cracking, "I believe I see now why you have brought me here. Chastain was buried in this cemetery and, as his partner in law—his partner in mind and habit too—I am also due in such a place as this."

The spirit made no sound as it passed beside Krow and pointed.

"I don't understand," Krow said, slowly continuing the climb, "between the m-morgue and this place...have I not yet seen enough? Have I—"

A sound silenced Krow. He stopped walking to listen. It was a muted grunting as if someone just over the hill were struggling against laborious work. *Who in their right mind would be working in a place such as this in the middle of the night?* Krow wondered. The answer that suggested itself was immediately disagreeable to Krow, but still, he was curious. A black tree with gnarled, spider-like limbs grew out of the top of a berm ahead. Whatever the sound was, it was coming from just the other side.

Krow ascended, grabbed ahold of the tree's most lateral branch, and pulled himself the rest of the way. He stared down the opposite hill and saw faint light. At the base was a tidy stone garden with a single tall headstone. And there was someone there, a prone shape with little discernible detail. The sound, however, was now much clearer. It was the hoarse, involuntary sobbing of a man.

The spirit, now at Krow's side, pointed down. It was a gradual descent, but Krow moved slowly. His legal mind raced to piece together the evidence of what he was about to witness. He could see only the back of the grave marker, but the dialogues in the district courthouse, the horror of the morgue, and the fact that Chastain was under the ground somewhere nearby—all argued the identity he would find on the front of that stone.

Krow turned back to the ghost. "Spirit, please," he cried out. "I don't need to see—" In turning, Krow lost his footing and slid on leaves, twigs, and snow the rest of the way down. He lay still for a moment, not daring to lift his head, not daring to see what must now be revealed. The urgent, convulsive, aching sobs were so much louder, so near.

Trembling, Krow lifted his head and saw the front of the gravestone. Upon the honed granite marker, engraved in dark letters was the name of Krow's nephew: FREDERICK BITHYWELL.

Krow reared up and fell backward. "Fred?" he cried. "But I can't... no, not Fred. Dear Fred!"

He looked up beseechingly at the spirit, answered only by a dim red glare. Then Krow turned to the man kneeling there. In the lantern's faint light, Krow recognized the man. It was Kevin Marwright. Krow leaped to his feet and began to back away. Then, he saw more writing on the headstone: *Beloved Husband.*

Krow looked to the stone and back at Kevin. The man, big man that he was, shook in his grief. In the lantern's light, Krow saw actually saw steam rising from the man's exposed neck.

"Do...you...see?" the spirit asked. The hooded specter loomed over Krow.

"No, Spirit, Fred was in good health," Krow spluttered, himself breaking down. "He was so young. He was in his prime."

"He battled depression...for many years," the spirit rasped. "He will...take...his...own...life."

Krow gasped, "No! No! Fred would never... could never—he was always so full of cheer and so jovial. Wait, was it this...this Kevin? Did he cause Fred's death?"

"Not...him," the spirit rasped. "You."

Krow coughed, bent double, and then screeched, "You lie, Spirit!"

The ghost's eyes flared a blazing blood red. Krow felt like he couldn't breathe. He thought surely those ethereal hands had appeared again, this time to throttle him. But no hands attended his throat. "Spirit, Spirit! I'm sorry, Spirit!" Krow cried. "I should never have said that. You cannot lie!"

"The love...they felt...was as real to them...as your love...for Annabelle was to you."

Krow looked down at Kevin and back up at the spirit. "How can you...how can you say that? Their love is a false thing!"

"Does that...look false...to you?" The spirit pointed the tip of his scythe blade toward Kevin.

Krow looked and then looked away. "Surely, surely, he is sincere," Krow said. "I cannot gainsay that. But so much sin! That is why I could never spend time with Fred. He was so stubborn about what he felt, so attached to this...this other man."

"You... Krow," the ghost hissed, "you convinced Fred...of his own...damnation."

Krow felt his blood boiling and yet, icy sweat dribbled down his back. "I did no such thing!" Krow shouted. "I just told Fred what the scriptures say... that he was living in sin."

"Do you...think...he didn't...know what the scriptures...say?"
The spirit's words came out with such heat that Krow stumbled
backward.

"Wait, wait!" Krow blurted to himself. "Did not Chastain tell
me one of you spirits would bear me nothing but malice? You,
spirit, you would have me believe that I caused my nephew to
take his own life because...because I didn't approve of his lifestyle. You...you..." Krow's voice trailed off.

There came a strange radiance from behind him, but that is
not what banished Krow's words. The spirit before him seemed
suddenly bent, leaning on its scythe as if exceedingly weary.

"No," Krow said, scarcely audible, "it was never about ap-
proving of Fred's lifestyle, was it, Spirit? Fred knew the scriptures and knew I tried...well, I tried to follow them. He didn't
need my approval. He needed...my love."

"NO!" a voice from behind thundered, and the entire graveyard filled with blinding light. The light seared through the Spirit of Christmas Yet to Come, shredding him away bit by bit like a
rotting scarecrow in a stiff wind.

As the spirit altogether dissipated, Krow thought he heard
unearthly laughter. Something took hold of Krow from behind
and spun him around, and there stood the first spirit, the Spirit of Christmas Past. Its armor glowed white hot and its eyes
bled tears of molten steel. "No, you shall not escape!" the spirit
raged. "It is too late! Too late! You must go to the fire and ice
and gnashing teeth!"

The spirit picked Krow up and threw him bodily into a
yawning hole in the ground. It was a grave! Krow screamed, but
did not hit bottom. There was no bottom.

Krow fell into darkness pierced only by spiraling blue
flames. He fell and fell. And into his mind, came the shadows
of that "other Krow" he had seen when the spirits had taken
him traveling. He saw that blurred countenance now as clearly
as in a mirror. Krow saw himself dressed in robes like the other
religious leaders and hissing curses at Jesus. He saw himself
spitting angry and striking Annabelle. He saw himself belittling

Bob Craggett, screaming out, "You're fired!" And finally, Krow saw himself in the morgue, sliding the long tray upon which his nephew's body lay, sliding it into its dark abode, slamming the silver door shut, and muttering, "You brought this on yourself."

Yourself.

YOURSELF.

The word amplified and deafened all other sound, and Krow fell. The blue flame flared up all around Krow. Dreadful, heavy chains reached up from below and took hold of him. The cold bit into him. It tore into his flesh. He struggled against the chains, clutched at them, tried to rip them free, but they burned his hands...or froze them. He couldn't tell, and it didn't matter. There was no question, no answer, no point in fighting inevitability. The light of the blue fire began to fade. The flames and chains dwindled down into a tangle of blankets.

STAVE V

THE END OF IT

B<small>LANKETS.</small>

Not flames, nor chains. Blankets. Krow's own blankets. His own floor. His own bed. The bedroom too was his very own.

Krow twisted out of the entangling blankets, leaped to his feet, and saw the clock. Best of all, there was the gift of time, time with which to make amends.

"All praise to Heaven!" Krow shouted. He dropped to his knees by the bed, shut his teary eyes tight, and prayed, "Never have I understood the reach of Grace until now! Such a man as I was, such a fool as I was, wasting the gifts I've been given as if they were of my own earning and for me alone! Man of law, humph! That man is dead. Good riddance to him. Lord of Mercy, forgive me. Create in me a clean heart. Let me share naught but Your love in this sin-scarred world that I used to darken with my very presence. Let me live with the spirit of Christmas Past, Present, and Future—all striving within me!

Wait, not so much the Past! The Past sought to do me evil, to restrain, and keep me there, but You, Lord, have released me! In Jesus' name, amen!"

Krow stood once more, saw the light of day outside, and ran to the window. It was early yet, but Krow threw up the sash. He drank in a deep draught of the frosty morning air. "Glorious snow! Purifies the world. Heavenly sky, feathery clouds—ah, all is Glory!"

From the corner of his eye, Krow perceived movement down the alley behind his home. "Hallo, there!" Krow cried out as a bundled boy began to pass his gate.

"You talking to me?" the young man asked.

"Why, yes," Krow said. "Can you...can you tell me what day is today?"

"What are you, kidding?"

"Brilliant boy," Krow said quietly to himself. "What a young man! So witty." He blinked and laughed heartily. "Yes, yes—I mean, no, I'm not kidding. What is the day?"

The boy squinted up at Krow. "Today? It's Christmas Day."

Krow gasped for joy. "I...I haven't missed it. I haven't. The powers of Heaven did it all in one night? Of course they did. There's no power greater! Hallo, young man!"

"You already said hello," the boy quipped.

"Well, hallo again and again," Krow said, "and a Merry Christmas thrown into the bargain!"

"Uh...Merry Christmas to you...uh, too."

"Say, young man," Krow said, the wheels in his mind turning and spinning with ideas, "I wonder if you'd consider doing me a favor. There's a twenty dollar bill in it for you."

"Twenty bucks? For real?"

"Yes, yes," Krow said. "What I need you to do is to head to the market square. Could you see if any of the open restaurants do catering? If you find one that does...wait, how do I do this?"

"I could call you on my cell," the lad suggested.

"Excellent! You do just that. If you find one and call me, I'll give you a second twenty dollar bill. If you call before I have to leave for church, I'll make it an even fifty!"

"Fifty dollars?" The young man had his phone out in an instant. Krow gave him his own number and said a silent prayer that his phone had battery life yet. The boy sped off, kicking up a rooster tail of fluffy snow.

Krow shut the window and clapped his hands. With a whoop, he raced from the bedroom into the sitting room. "Ha!" he crowed. "There's the chair I sat in. There's the chair that Chastain did *not* sit in! It's all true. It all happened. Heavenly Glory! Ha, ha, ha!"

For a man such as Ebenezer Krow who had not used a true laugh for anything but courtroom histrionics, it was really quite a spectacular laugh! Krow grabbed his own sides and guffawed until he was red in the face and dizzy. Steadying himself along the wall, he made his merry way back into the bedroom and dressed for the day.

Oh, yes, he did. Krow put on a suit with bright red vest beneath, an overcoat with a green scarf, and an old top hat he found on a high dusty shelf in the far back of the closet. He did not take his usual walking stick. The cane with the crow was destined for Tuesday morning's garbage pick-up. Instead, he selected a very plain, hand-carved stave that he'd purchased many years before at a local craft show.

A pulsing chime momentarily stopped the procession, and Krow hurried back to the sitting room and grabbed up his phone. "Hallo!" he shouted.

It was the lad from the gate. He had come through. He had found a 24-Hour Diner that was willing to cater, even on Christmas Day. Krow took down the diner's number and told the young man to come back by the house to pick up his earnings and more besides.

Krow called the diner, ordered such a Christmas feast as the Spirit of Christmas Present would approve. He gave his credit card for the bill and substantial tip. He hung up and laughed again. "Bob Craggett, if only I could see your face when the feast arrives!"

Just then, the church bells of the Queen City began to ring. Krow practically danced down the stairwell without it issuing so much as the tiniest creak of complaint. Out the door, into the snow, he went. He waited at the gate for the young man to come back, which he did presently, and handed him a one hundred dollar bill. "Merry Christmas!" Krow told the boy.

Eyes as big as ostrich eggs, the boy heartily returned the wish and ran off. Careful not to slip and slide, Krow set about at a brisk pace in the other direction, for he had a special errand at the church.

Krow found the walk itself exhilarating. Every inhaled breath was a frosty pleasure, and every exhale was a marvel of abstract art. But if you think that Krow was unaware of the people moving hither and thither around him, you'd only need to remove the cotton from your ears. Krow looked each person in the eye, gave a glorious, contagious, glowing smile, and wished Merry Christmas to all.

One "Merry Christmas," however, went awry at first. A familiar couple began to return Krow's greeting, but their words caught in their throats. Krow immediately knew them, for they were the couple who had come into his office before closing and asked for a donation to their charities. As they passed him, Krow spun and caught them up. "My good friends," Krow said, "I hope your mission for the New Hampshire Food Bank and Good Shepherd Inner City Provisions was a grand success. You are doing good work. Merry Christmas to you both!"

"Mr. Krow?" the woman named Lucille gasped, eying him with suspicious curiosity.

"Yes," Krow replied, "Ebenezer Krow is my name, and I fear I made it very unpleasant to you yesterday. Allow me to beg your pardon for my crass words and terrible lack of munificence. I wonder...I wonder if you would have the goodness to accept—" Here, Krow huddled the pair close in and whispered to them.

The dapper gentleman named Clinton stood up suddenly, blinking as if he'd been blinded by a glare off the snow. "Mr. Krow?" he said. "My good sir, are you quite serious?"

"I am," Krow said. "Not a dollar less. There are a great many back payments included in it. Far too many, God forgive me. Will you do me that favor?"

Lucille stood up on tip toe and kissed Krow on the cheek. "I had you all wrong," she said, beaming. "I... I don't know what to say to such generosity."

"You need not say anything at all," Krow said. "Come and see me at the firm this week. Will you come?"

"We will," Clinton and Lucille said together. And it was clear they were in earnest.

"Thank you both dearly," Krow said. "I am in your debt. Ha, ha! Both figuratively and literally. Thank you, a thousand times, thank you. God's richest blessings upon you."

The chiming bells of St. Nicodemus called Krow away and, for a man with a cane, he made quite a hasty passage to the church. Removing his hat as he entered, Krow smoothly took a seat in the very back. It was an unusual place for him as elders in the church had special seating near the front. But on this Christmas Day, Krow knew no better place to be.

After the announcements ended, the choir emerged and began their spectacular performance of "Angels We Have Heard On High." Krow sang at the top of his lungs, weeping as he belted out the chorus, "Gloria, in excelsis Deo!" He knew now precisely to Whom he was singing.

Keeping his peripheral vision trained on the church doors, Krow continued to sing. The doors opened, and in walked the young woman decked out in black and chrome, backpack slung upon her back. She took her seat on the edge of the back pew, not eight feet from Krow.

When Gladys Perliman appeared, she knelt and said to the visitor. "I'm sorry to disturb you, but I don't know you."

"I...I'm Sarah," she replied, ducking her head.

"Welcome to St. Nicodemus," Mrs. Perliman said, "But this is a—"

"This is the pastor's wife," Krow told Sarah, "and she's quite right. This isn't a regular service. This is Christmas Service!"

"Elder Krow," Mrs. Perliman said, cheeks reddening. "I'm quite sure—"

"I'm quite sure as well," Krow intoned. "I'm sure that for such a special service, Sarah will want a much better seat." Krow took Sarah's hand, drew her to her feet, and then out the other side of the pew. He led her to the front of the church, bowed, and gestured for Sarah to be seated...in the Elders' Section.

Krow sat beside her and whispered to her, "I'm sure this all seems terribly awkward, but I wanted to apologize for my behavior last night at The Bleak House Tavern."

Recognition dawned on Sarah's face. "You? You were so mean."

Krow bowed his head and, when he looked up, his eyes glistened. "I was far out of line," he said. "Please forgive me. Seeing you here at my church makes me so happy I could burst, but will you stay for the rest of the service?"

Sarah blinked. "I came here today," she said, her voice faltering, "hoping...well, I didn't know what to expect, but yes, I'll stay."

Krow clapped his hands, earning a few glances from the pew in front of theirs. "And I wonder, will you and your friends meet again at the tavern tonight? I should like to buy the first round."

Sarah smiled, and it was to Krow, a bewildering yet beautiful sight. "You're weird," she said, "but, yeah, I'll call the crew. We'll be there."

Krow made to reply, but immediately became aware that he was about to blubber and that might just prove "too weird" for Sarah. So, Krow sang instead. When the song ended, and the choir made to leave, Krow interrupted the sacred silence and called out, "Bravo, Choir! As an elder, I can say I have rarely been moved like I have by your song today! Linger, and let's have another song!"

The choir master looked as though he'd swallowed a cold fish. Krow turned to the congregation, "What do you say, St. Nicodemus, would you like to hear more singing?"

At first, the crowd sat in stunned silence. But then, a teenager in the third row started clapping. "Yeah, man!" he shouted. "Let's hear some more. It's Christmas!"

Whistles came from all over the congregation and people began to cheer. Someone cried out, "How about 'Oh, Holy Night?'"

Grinning, the choir master gestured for his troops to return, and they began a luminous rendition of "Oh, Holy Night" that left two-thirds of the congregation in tears.

When the service ended, Krow bid Sarah a Merry Christmas and then scurried for the church side door. He had no time for the criticisms or questions of the other elders. His stomach churning, knotting up with all manner of anxiety, Krow vanished down the lane behind the church on a long-overdue mission.

* * *

Bob Craggett heard the doorbell. Oh, did he ever. It sounded as if someone were trying to ring it off the wall with a terrible urgency.

"Well, who could that be?" Bob asked. "Everyone's already here."

"I have no idea," Mrs. Craggett said, straightening a very Christmassy dish towel on the oven door handle. "Kay, would you mind seeing who's at the door?"

"Okay," came Kay's answer from some distance above. Bob and his wife heard their daughter bound down the steps. They heard the door open. They heard a muted conversation. Some man was at the door by the sound of the voice.

Then, they heard Kay, "Mom, Dad, I...uh, I think you should come up here."

Exchanging nervous glances, husband and wife ascended the stairs to the front door. They saw a van parked outside the fence. Its double back doors were thrown open, and a couple of ladies were unloading huge, foil-covered pans. A man wearing a jacket with a T&C Diner patch emblazoned upon its lapel was holding out a clipboard. "Are you Bob Craggett?" he asked.

"Yes, but I didn't order any—"

"Just need you to sign here, sir," he said, handing Bob the clipboard and a pen.

"But what...what am I signing for?"

"Christmas Dinner," the man replied joyfully. "And it's quite a meal too. I hope you have some big appetites in your family."

"Dinner?" Bob said quizzically.

"Christmas Dinner," Mrs. Craggett said, turning with a warm expression to her husband. "Bob, is this your doing?"

"On my life, it is not," Bob said. "You know how I value your cooking, and we haven't the money for—"

"Already been paid for," the man said. "Tipped nicely too. So could you just sign here so we can bring everything in?"

"Already been paid?" Bob asked. He signed the document on the clipboard. "Who bought all this for us?"

"Thank you, sir," the man said. Then over his shoulder, he called, "Okay, Linda, Taryn, start bringing in the sides." He turned back to Bob and said, "A gentleman purchased this grand feast for you, but he wishes to remain anonymous."

"I'm flummoxed," Bob said. "What should we do?"

"I say we accept this unlooked-for-gift," Mrs. Craggett said, "and I say we have the best Christmas meal ever!"

"Where's the kitchen, ma'am?" the man asked.

"Down the stairs and you'll see it on the right."

As the three caterers took turns traversing back and forth from van to kitchen, the rest of the Craggetts assembled in a line upon the stairs.

Every time a foil-covered pan passed by, Little Tom piped up, "Whazzat?"

And the answers came cheerily: mashed potatoes, corn-bread and sausage stuffing, green beans, broccoli casserole, candied yams, pudding, cranberry sauce, carrots, and ham.

The two T&C Diner ladies worked together to carry in a very large pan, the foil not hiding the bulbous shape beneath.

"Is that the turkey?" Tom asked.

"Why, yes, it is, young man," Linda replied.

"It's HUGE!" Tom exclaimed.

"It is indeed," said Taryn, "Twenty pounds of golden good-ness!"

"Twenty pounds!" Bob blurted. "That would feed an army!"

"This feast is enough food for twenty-five," Linda said as they carefully navigated the stairs with that monster bird.

"Twenty-five people?" Bob echoed. "That gives me an idea." He turned and gathered his family into a huddle. "Let's each think of two or three people we might invite to join us for this unprecedented Christmas Dinner. Can we each do that?"

"I can!" Kay said, whipping out her phone.

"I can too," Mark said, racing up the stairs.

"That's a wonderful idea, Bob," Mrs. Craggett said.

"Well, we've been blessed," he replied. "Best we bless others!"

"What about the Taylors?" Mrs. Craggett asked. "They've seemed so lonely since their kids moved away."

"Brilliant!" Bob proclaimed.

The Craggett family had no trouble finding dinner guests, and when five o'clock came 'round, their home was overflowing with such satisfying joy—satisfaction of appetite and heart—that the Ghost of Christmas Present must certainly have been, well... present.

* * *

Krow sat in the back of a cab, and his thoughts raced.

"'Scuse me, sir," the cabbie said, "but the meter's running."

"That's all right," Krow replied with a deep exhale. "Do you mind waiting, parked right here? I'm not sure how long I'll be, but the meter doesn't concern me."

"Certainly, sir."

Krow emerged from the back of the cab, shut the door, and approached a gated driveway. Lost in thought, he kept walking until he smacked unceremoniously into the gate. He bounced back a step, rubbing his forehead and nose. "Forgot," he muttered, "I can't walk through things anymore. Won't I look lovely?"

Krow parted the gates, walked up the drive, and stood on

the doorstep of the colonial home. Taking a deep breath, he rang the bell.

A tall young man opened the door, and Krow could hear "Jingle Bell Rock" playing from somewhere inside.

"Can I help you?" he asked, taking a somewhat defensive stance and pulling the door shut behind him.

"I hope so," Krow said. "I know it's a busy day for everyone, but I was wondering if I might speak with your mother, Annabelle Prentice, or at least that was her name when we were friends many years ago."

"It's D'inardi now. Could I have your name? I'll go ask her."

"Ebenezer Krow," he replied. "Thank you, lad."

Krow kneaded his fingers with his thumbs and felt his stomach continue to tighten. What would she say? How would she react? Krow usually prepared methodically for a case, but he found no precedent for his current situation.

Annabelle D'inardi appeared in the doorway. She looked much the way she had when the Spirit of Christmas Past had brought Krow to this house, a vision of seven years prior. Her eyes were dark and mysterious, her lashes still long. But her hair had gone silver, and she wore it long with an unusual braid hanging down beside her left eye.

"Of all the surprises I might expect on Christmas Day," she said, "I wouldn't have dreamed you'd come to call."

"I would have called first," Krow stammered. "But I don't know the number."

"I'm astonished a man of your resourcefulness didn't just look it up online." She crossed her arms and waited. Krow noticed that the music inside had stopped.

Krow took off his hat and fidgeted with its brim. "All the same," he said, "what I've come here to say should be face-to-face, not with the comfortable distance of a cell network."

"Whatever you've come to say, Ebenezer," she said, "you'd best get on with it. It's cold out here, and the hours of Christmas Day are precious."

"Yes," Krow replied. "Yes, they are. Perhaps I should have

chosen another time to come. I'm sure you and your husband and family have many warm plans for today and tonight."

"My husband?" Annabelle echoed, nibbling at her bottom lip. "Richard lost his battle with cancer three years ago."

"Oh," Krow replied. "Oh, I am very sorry. Truly, I am, Annabelle. Forgive me...forgive me for coming. I will return at a better time; perhaps, after the New Year." He turned to leave.

"Wait," Annabelle said. "Wait, Ebenezer. How can I be so cold-hearted on Christmas? Come, say your piece. Let's go inside by the fire."

Krow followed her and, as he stepped over the threshold of the front door, he felt he'd crossed a sacred boundary: a home built by husband, wife, and children. A precious sanctuary of memories and life. He was a stranger here. He felt like a trespasser.

She led him into a round sitting room where a fire burned steadily beneath a hearth adorned with more than a dozen family photographs, some of toddlers. A distant part of Krow registered that Annabelle had a few grandchildren now. He looked away from the pictures and waited until Annabelle gestured for him to take a seat. It was a long couch, and they sat at opposite ends.

"On the cab ride over here," Krow began, "I had a dozen different ways to begin this conversation. Now I know they were all worthless. So, I'll come straight to the point. Annabelle, I am sorry."

Annabelle looked up sharply. "Sorry? For what? Surely, you don't mean...that was thirty years ago. We were kids."

Krow shook his head. "You are a resilient woman," he said, "and clearly you've recovered and even flourished. But there are some acts in life, some deeds committed, that even time cannot sweep away. Annabelle, I am sorry for throwing away our relationship that day in the park. I was bitter, jealous, judgmental, and heartless. I shouted in the face of your tears, your hurt. I added to your wounds. I called you 'spoiled' and accused you of every sin I could think of. I was a fool, a wicked man. The very fact that

it took me these many years to realize is a testament to how de-
praved a man I was. Oh, Annabelle, I was so wrong."

He began to weep, a slow churning sob, but gaining momentum. Annabelle sat very still. She too had tears, but they
were cold and quiet, running in single thin streaks down her
expressionless face.

"Annabelle, I am so sorry for all that I did, all that I said. I
was a cold, lifeless man. That day haunted me for thirty years,
and I deserved all of it and more. But you...you did not deserve
any of it. I know it is far too little to apologize, and far too late to
change anything; but I beg you to forgive me. I am not the man
I was. By God's grace, I am not...the man I was."

From the corner of his eye, Krow saw two little people in
footy pajamas peering around a doorjamb, but he didn't care.
Were the whole world to know of all his blackest sins, it would be
no less than he deserved.

"You hurt me that day, Ebenezer," she said very quietly. "I
was so intensely in love with you that your rejection felt like being torn limb from limb. And, do you know what? For the longest
time, I blamed myself! I called myself 'soiled, spoiled, wretched,
lascivious, and... worthless.' And why? Because the man I loved
saw me that way. But I healed, Ebenezer. I healed, and I swore
that I would never let another man govern the way I see myself. And I never did. Not that Richard ever tried. He was a dear
man, a loving husband and father...and he was my companion
through life."

"Good," Krow said, his heart sinking. "You deserved better,
better than...me."

"I don't understand, Ebenezer," Annabelle said, crossing her
arms. "Why do you seek forgiveness? Why now after all this
time? What does it matter, really? Never mind! I don't need to
know. To be honest, I've felt sorry for you. Whereas I healed and
grew, you never did. Yes, I'll admit it: I drove by your firm many
times with a mind to take you to task. But every time I did, I
couldn't help but feel that you were already paying penance, day
after lonely day, year after hollow year. Very well, Ebenezer, I

forgive you. You seem heartily sorry, but even if you did not, I would forgive you still. No one should have to bear a burden like this as long as you have."

She stood and gestured for him to stand again, for departure was near at hand.

"Annabelle," Krow said as Annabelle walked him to the door, "thank you for your mercy and forgiveness. I don't deserve either, but I am utterly grateful. If there is ever anything at all I can do for you or your family, please call. I'm sure you've seen the number on the billboard downtown."

"You mean the flaring yellow six-foot numbers?" she asked.

"Yes," Krow said, face reddening. "Those are the ones. But, I mean it, if you ever need anything day or night, call. If no one is there, it forwards the call directly to my phone."

She opened the door for Krow, and he took a few steps outside. "Goodbye, Ebenezer," Annabelle said. "I don't believe I will have any need to call you or see you again, but it was good of you to come. You were right when you said, 'There are some acts in life, some deeds committed, that even time cannot sweep away.' Seeing you today has torn the scab off of a very old wound, but maybe now, it will fully heal."

She closed the door, and Ebenezer Krow leaned a little more heavily on his walking stick as he slowly made his way back to the waiting cab.

* * *

"Who was that, Mom?" Ryan, Annabelle's oldest son asked the moment the door shut.

She sighed. "A very, very old friend," she replied. "No one to waste a thought about. Now, run along to the kitchen get those pumpkin pies out of the fridge."

"Okay, Mom," Ryan said, but he watched her suspiciously until the end of the hall where he turned the corner.

Annabelle didn't turn on the light in the stairwell as she ascended. She didn't turn on her bedroom light either. She sat on the bed in the blue-tinted twilight. She opened a shallow drawer on her bedside table and reached within. After a few moments of fishing around, her hand came back with a very small box. She opened it and stared at the ring within. It had taken divers with metal detectors the better part of a weekend to find it, and Annabelle had intended to sell it and give the money to charity. Somehow, she never managed to do so.

* * *

The cab dropped Krow off in a nice neighborhood in Hooksett. Krow paid his fee, gave the cabbie a large tip, and wished him a Merry Christmas.

"I am Hindu," the cabbie replied, "but I thank you anyway. I know you mean me good will."

"I do," Krow said. "And thank you for understanding. I'll be a few hours here. Can you wait that long? I don't mind the money. And I'll certainly tip extra."

The cabbie finished counting the bills Krow had given him. "Oh, I can wait," he said. "Take your time."

The cab idling across the street, Krow meandered between parked cars and made his way to his nephew's front door. The house was lit up but not on the outside. Various shades of golden light shone out from the inside as if the sun itself was a special guest at the party. It was still relatively early in the evening, so Krow thought that maybe he'd have a chance to talk to his nephew privately. Of course, the modest collection of cars parked along the sidewalk suggested otherwise.

With a deep breath, Krow depressed the doorbell. Krow heard someone shout inside, and soon, the door opened. A young woman in a dark red dress stood on the landing. *Mary was her name,* Krow thought. "Yes?" she said. "May I help you?"

Krow removed his hat and gave a quick bow. "Yes, yes, I hope so. I'm here for the party. Am I late?"

"No, no," she replied. "A few of us came early to help with the food."

"Oh, good," Krow said. "Could you see if Fred is about? I'd like to talk to him for a moment before I come in."

"He's about, all right," the woman said. "He's been a veritable whirlwind around here. I'll see if I can find him. Who...who should I say...I mean, I'm afraid I don't know you."

"Just tell him his uncle is here," Krow said.

Mary disappeared within, leaving the door open but a crack. Krow heard voices and some kind of commotion. The door flew open, and Fred stood there, gaping. "I...I don't believe it," he said. "Uncle Ebenezer?"

"Yes, Nephew," Krow said. "I have come for the dinner party. Will you let me in?"

Let him in! Fred nearly knocked the screen door off its hinges, for he couldn't get it open fast enough. His face aglow, he offered his uncle a hand. Krow refused it, instead gathering his nephew in for an embrace.

"I am sorry, Fred," Krow said into his nephew's ear. "I am sorry for what I said to you yesterday, for what I said about Christmas. All of that was hogwash of the worst kind."

"Uncle Ebenezer?" Fred said, separating their embrace to arm's length. "Are you...feeling well?"

"I am now," Krow said. "But more than all my reprehensible words yesterday, I am sorry for years of pushing you away, years of judgment, and years of neglect. But I should like to remedy that, if you'll let me. I was thinking that perhaps we could find time for a long lunch once a month. And Kevin too, if he can get away."

Fred blinked and cried, grinned and gaped. "Are you...certain? For years you've had nothing but disdain for—"

"More like years of insecurity, Fred," Krow said. "But I should like to get to know you—and Kevin—much better, if you'll both welcome my company."

"Welcome? Yes!" Fred exclaimed. "But... the sudden change? How? I mean, what about your church and your scriptures?"

Krow nodded, for he understood his nephew's disconnect, and he understood the role he himself had played in it. "Fred, the church is full of broken and searching souls. We're hardly perfect, but there is a lot of good there too. And I intend to work tirelessly to amplify all that is good. As for the Bible, I believe it. There's really no getting around what God clearly presents in His Word. But, now more than ever, I understand the meaning of Grace. May God forgive me for not showing you and so many others the Grace that has been shown to me. Grace I never merited and never deserved."

Fred's face reddened with emotion. His eyes glistened. His voice caught when he tried to speak. He hugged his uncle one more time and then cleared his throat. "You have made me...so glad, Uncle," he said. "Come, I can't keep you standing here."

Fred led Krow up a short flight of stairs. At the top, Kevin was waiting.

There came an awkward, frozen moment when Krow and Kevin stared at each other with Fred in between.

"Were you listening?" Fred asked.

"Heard every word," Kevin replied.

Krow took a step forward, held out his hand to Kevin, and said, "I'm terribly sorry to you too, Kevin. I'd be grateful for a chance to get to know you."

Kevin's eyes lingered on Krow's outstretched hand. "You know," Kevin said, "in this house, we don't shake hands...with family. We just hug...it...out."

And before Krow could utter a word, he was smothered by the much larger man and then by Fred as well.

That night, Krow and Fred and Kevin, as well as all the dinner guests enjoyed a sumptuous feast, continuous Christmas carols, festive games, and as warm and glowing a time as any could remember. At long last, Krow reported to Fred with regret that he had to depart. He had another party, of sorts, to attend.

"When can we talk again?" Fred asked.

"Why not this week?" Krow replied. "See what works well for you and Kevin, and I will make myself available."

When Krow sat down in the back of the taxi, the cab driver said, "Sir...you've accumulated quite a bill with all this. I'd hate to take so much money from you, especially on your Christmas Day, but—"

"Don't say it," Krow insisted. "I'll happily pay the full tab, as promised, and a large tip for your catering to my needs and likely missing out on many other opportunities."

The cabbie smiled broadly. "Where to now?"

"The Bleak House Tavern," Krow replied. "And, while I won't need a ride home from there, you are more than welcome to join me and...some friends for a Christmas nightcap."

"Right kind of you, sir," he said. "Perhaps, I will."

Krow let his head fall back on the headrest and stared up at the night sky. It had been a very long time since he last gazed up at the stars with the wonder he now felt. Perhaps, not since he was a child. Krow was lost in thought until his phone rang. He looked at the screen but didn't recognize the number.

He pressed the green connect icon and said, "Merry Christmas!"

The voice from the phone made his heart skip a beat. "I am sorry for calling so late, Ebenezer," Annabelle said, "but...I wonder if you might have time this week to discuss a case."

"You aren't suing me, are you?" Krow asked. His words were full of jesting, but his mind was quite sincerely unsure.

"No," she replied. "At least, not at present. No, I need your assistance. Can we meet?"

Krow said that they could indeed. He let Annabelle pick the time and place. When their conversation ended, Krow quickly added Annabelle's number to his contacts. He clicked the save icon and whispered, "Will wonders never cease?"

* * *

The next morning, Krow awoke very early to the chimes of his phone's alarm. He sat up, feeling a bit groggy, and muttered, "Probably shouldn't have had that third pint at The Bleak House."

But then, he remembered his plan for the day and that had him up, dressed, and eager for the office in just a few minutes.

Krow arrived first at the firm, disarmed the security system, and raced inside. He proceeded to his desk, booted up the computer, and made a few very necessary adjustments. Then, like a smug spider having spun a very large web indeed, Krow waited.

Other employees arrived on time, as usual. Krow said nothing. A few others wandered in right at the stroke of nine. Krow said nothing.

At ten past the hour, no Bob.

At quarter past the hour, no Bob.

Finally, at twenty-one minutes past nine, Bob whisked into the firm. He had his coat and scarf hung in an instant. And with his hair sticking up behind his ear, and his tie hanging at a very unusual angle, Bob sat down at his small desk and set about to work.

"Mr. Craggett!" growled Krow. "At my desk!"

A hush fell over the entire firm. The other clerks and assistants watched Bob trudge to Krow's massive black walnut desk. He stood there as if facing a firing squad.

Krow leaned forward and gave the best scowl he could manage, endeavoring to capture the flavor of his former self. "Mr. Craggett, you are late. Quite late."

"I am very sorry, sir," Bob said, downcast. "I missed the first bus, but it was my delay that caused it. No excuse."

"You are right about that, Bob," Krow growled. "There is no excuse whatsoever."

"We were making rather merry yesterday," Bob said quietly. "It's only once a year. I will not repeat the mistake. And, I'll stay late tonight to make amends."

"You will not repeat the mistake," Krow said, "nor will you be staying late tonight, or any night as far as I'm concerned. I'll tell you, my friend, I cannot tolerate this work ethic and attitude any longer. And therefore..." Krow was up in a flash, rounded the desk, and came at Bob with such fervor that poor Bob nearly fainted.

"Therefore!" Krow repeated, taking hold of Bob's shoulders. "I am giving you...a promotion and a raise!"

Bob swayed a little. He saw an old metal stapler on Krow's desk and thought momentarily about knocking Krow unconscious with it. At least then he could call the police and tell them to bring a straightjacket for his employer who had clearly lost his mind.

"Merry Christmas to you, Bob!" Krow shouted with such warmth and joviality that his words could not be mistaken. "A merrier Christmas, Bob, my most loyal and hardworking friend, than I have given you since you first came to the firm! And long overdue! I am raising your salary and promoting you this instant."

At this, Krow let go of his bewildered employee and stepped to the side so that he could see all of his gawking employees. "My dear friends," he said, his voice booming, "I thank all of you for your dedication to this firm. It gives me great pleasure to announce that I am hereby making Bob Craggett a full partner in our practice! The sign will be changed within the week to read, 'Krow and Craggett.' Please welcome our new partner!"

The ground floor of the firm exploded in applause, shouts, and whistles. The clapping lasted over a minute. Bob, slack-jawed and blinking back tears, turned to his employer and said, "Partner?"

"Yes, yes, Bob," Krow said, "and in more ways than one. Together we are going to overhaul the firm's insurance package. Together, we are going to help that precious family of yours overcome every obstacle. We'll discuss the particulars over a Christmas brunch at The Bleak House Tavern."

"Brunch?" Bob said, "but... work?"

"Can wait," Krow said. Then, broadcasting to the whole office once more, he announced, "The offices of Krow and Craggett will be closed for the remainder of the day! Go and be with the ones you love! And, if the mood strikes you, come join us at The Bleak House Tavern for a mighty brunch!"

The office cheered once more. Bob took hold of Krow's upper arm. "I don't...I don't know what to say. 'Thank you' seems so inadequate."

"It's far more than adequate, Bob, my good man. Now, let's help our dedicated staff find their way out the door, shall we? We cannot get to the bacon and hash browns too soon, can we, Bob Craggett?"

His eyes glimmering, Bob could only smile in return.

* * *

Krow was better than his word. He did everything he promised to do and so much more that I could scarcely try to relate it all in a vast series of books. And to Tom Craggett, Bob's precious *Little Bear,* who did not die, Krow became a second father. But, since the name Big Bear was taken, Tom took to calling Krow *Grand Bear.*

Ebenezer Krow became as good a family man, as good an employer, as good a friend as the Queen City could know—or any city, for that matter. At Krow's leading, the sanctuary of St. Nicodemus was ever-filled with singing, especially at Christmas. And the dear old church became such a welcoming and loving place that it had to open several new campuses across Manchester.

Krow had no more visits from spirits, specters, or angels—none that he could see anyway. Krow himself might disagree on that last, for he did have visits from Annabelle. Quite a few, leading eventually to their wedding. And to Krow, Annabelle would always be an angel.

Ever after, it was always said of him that, if any person alive possessed the method, Ebenezer Krow knew best—not how to keep Christmas—but to give it away. May that also be said of each of us. And, as Little Bear observed, "God bless us, and all the people of the world!"

THE END

ACKNOWLEDGEMENTS

To Mary Lu, Kayla, Tommy, Bryce, and Rachel, thank you for sharing so many Christmas Eves and allowing me to include "A Christmas Carol" in our traditions. Every word that I write belongs equally to you all. I love you. P.S. The George C. Scott version RULES!

To my extended family and friends, bless you for supporting me over the years as I've been on this crazy writing adventure. You all know the ups and downs of LIFE we've all been through together. Without you, not only would I never have written a book, but I daresay I might have ended up in a padded room!

To Laura G. Johnson, thank you for your editing expertise and prayerful insights. This is a story I always wanted to write, but it wasn't until writing it that I realized that there were heart issues that needed to come to light. You helped me to sort out some of those and sharpened up the story incredibly well.

To Caleb Havertape, your talent has graced my book covers for several years now. You ROCKED this cover! I can't imagine having a different artist. Thank you.

To Malachi Armas, thank you for the splendid interior design. You blow me away with your craft. I am in your debt.

To Alaina Piek, thank you for the timely analysis of A Christian's Carol. I learned a lot from you, and ultimately, this is a better story because of your influence.

To Keith Alan Robinson, thank you for the stroke of midnight insights. I think your help with "that scene" really clarified what I was intending to accomplish through the scene. I owe you one.

To Christopher Hopper, thank you for your perspectives when I was just formulating the story. Not just your ideas (which really helped me) but also who you are as a person. Iron sharpens Iron.

To Joey and Kim Shell for letting me haunt your beach home to write Stave 3! You provided amazing hospitality and a refuge in the wake of hurricane Florence. Thank you.

To the generous Patrons who support my work financially (and often prayerfully), thank you for making this book and every book a dream come true. Please see your names below and know that you are a HUGE part of everything I write. I will never be able to thank you enough.

The Pantheon of Patreon Patrons:
• Abigail Geiger
• Alexandra Johnson
• Alyssa and Caleb Hoeksema
• Ama Lane
• Amanda Straffin
• Andrea Hinkson
• Andrea Martinson
• Arikabart Bartholomew
• Ashton Becht
• Braden Mabry
• Brionna Wheaton
• Bryce Spitzer
• Charles Michael Howard
• Chris Harvey
• Christian Humbert
• Christopher Abbott
• Christopher Hopper
• Clinton McDonald
• Cody Pennington
• David Larson
• Dayman Hartman
• Elizabeth (eBeth) Hornberger
• Emily Bagenstos
• Eric Guglielmo

- Erica Smith
- Erin Primrose
- Ethan Havener
- Hailey Fisher
- Hannah Worthington
- Harvey Williams
- Josiah Mann
- Kaylin Calvert
- Laure Hittle
- Liane and Hannah Agro
- Logan Brown
- Luke Dyess
- Mary Lyall
- Matt Toews
- Melinda Limantoro
- Micah Reninger
- Michael Harper
- Michael Schneider
- Michelle White
- Nathan R. Petrie
- Nicole Burnett
- Noah Cutting
- Peter Vaughn
- R.M. Archer
- Raymond Caso
- Rebecca Abrams
- Rebekah Main
- Robert McCarville
- Ruth Geiger
- Ryan Paige Howard
- Sam Jenne
- Samuel Stocking
- Sarah Bushey
- Schyler Ford
- Sean Lyall
- Shane Kent
- Starr Family
- Stephen Larson
- Zach Martin

Last but certainly not least, thank you to Charles Dickens whose story has had (and continues to have) the most pleasantly haunting impact on so many.

OTHER BOOKS
YOU MIGHT LIKE...

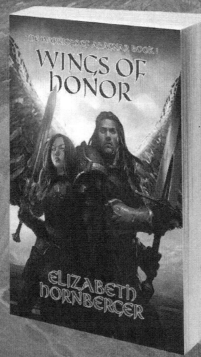

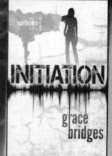

WHISPERS FROM THE DEPTHS

"She who wields the waters for revenge drowns herself tenfold."

a thrilling debut by **C.W. Briar**

arising 2019

Oath of Shepherds

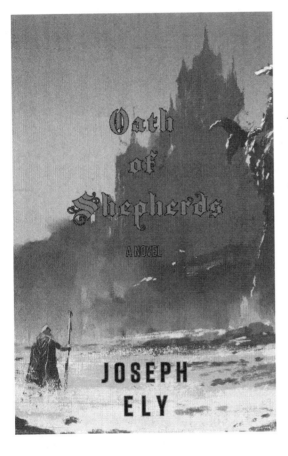

A kingdom unraveled.
A warrior bound.
A quest traveled.
A magic found.
The world will never be
the same when
kingdoms collide.
Faith will be found
where the Oath of
Shepherds abide.

Summer 2019

Follow debut author, Joseph Ely, at:

www.kensingtonrealm.com

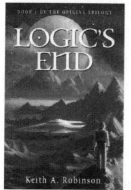

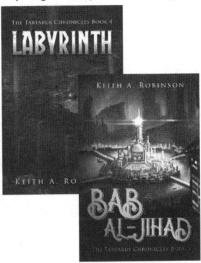